DEAD MAN SWITCH

I0654986

Ross Davies

COPYRIGHT

ACKNOWLEDGEMENTS

I would like to thank everyone. I know everyone is such a broad term, but I truly mean it. Everyone I've met, even those I only met for a second or have known my entire life, thank you. I'd like to thank you for the influence, the experience, and the memories.

I would like to thank my family for the unending support and understanding. I would like to thank my Downpatrick population, every friend I met there, every day I spent there, to all the groups I lived with and how every one of you helped me become who I am today.

Thank you to those who believed in me and even those who didn't. Every shred of emotion invested in me helped me get here.

I love you, all of you, and you know who you are and even if you don't, I promise, you will.

Sincerely,
Ross Davies

THE FIRST HOUR

Polluted stench I smell, that's all I could smell. Lying on the floor of a back-end rest stop washroom wasn't my idea of a perfect vacation, especially not with two bullet wounds.

Well, I mean it could be worse, I could be dead.

The bullets didn't hit anything necessary, or at least I hope they didn't. Now I'm lying on glass and the only thing between me and the bastard who shot me is a sheet metal stall door. Wait to see his feet, I thought, one bullet for his ankle and the other for his skull. When that fucker drops, the skull fragments are going to shred the tile wall.

The blood from my wounds slowly seeps out and begins to stain my new white shirt. Well fuck, bullet holes add decoration, but the blood just pisses me off. First, it is nearly impossible to get out; second, it's hard as hell to explain. A piece of mirror shatters with a loud crunch under his foot. The sound sends shivers through me. It wakes me,

I'm aware of what's happened and now very ready. Don't think.

React now because I've just been shot.

I have only moments to retaliate with accuracy and nothing less or I'm to die here.

His impression of designer leather shoes stick to floor cured like Coca-Cola in an unwashed movie theater. I now wait patiently as he makes a pathetic attempt to slowly tiptoe his way towards my small chamber.

I'll wait until I see his ankle, or, just maybe, he'll check under the stall, so I can see his face. Every single step he takes is followed by the loud crunching of glass. Every step sends even smaller pieces of glass streaming across the inky black floor, and with every crunch the fragments tear across the opaque surface. Petrified, my breaths are silent and with my eyes I cover every direction with a lidless stare, all I do is wait and watch the floor. The obsidian tiled floor, the surface, covered in thousands of crystals, resembling the sky of a cold winter night, the darkest night you can imagine. The streaming

pieces of glass are like shooting stars tearing across its cloudless surface.

Somehow, I'm calm, even as I bleed out.

Then it clouds as I see a foot, a brown leather shoe. Fuck assumptions, this guy has leather shoes. Like a blinding light, I see sock between designer black pants and expensive brown leather shoe. Smile, my gun raised, I close an eye.

Breathe in and squeeze.

In a liquid flash, his ankle is gone.

A scream, and then a slender face hits my sky. I see widened eyes behind four-hundred-dollar sunglasses.

I see a grim image of pain, surprise, and knowing the end.

He sees my smile.

Desperately, he begins to force himself from the ground, hoping to get out of my view, while my finger begins to squeeze the trigger.

Thunderous, my last bullet enters a millimeter above his brow. Just like I said, the wall under the sink shatters from the skull fragment projectiles.

Sick. As I stand, my clip bounces from the floor. I quickly feed the gun a fresh magazine.

The sound of the clip bouncing sends a shrill echo through the washroom and as it stills, the silence resumes. Reaching for the stall door, I sigh. I step over my kill and smile,

"Bet you didn't think that was going to fucking happen...now did you?" I chuckle.

I kneel down, hovering over him and I pick up his gun, pocketing it. This is the moment of recognition. My thoughts are bothering me. They're ripping deep and telling me things I don't like.

This guy is familiar. I know him, but from where, where in hell have, I seen him? Come on, think, where the fuck have, I seen him? Reaching into his pants, I frantically pull his wallet out. Five hundred dollars, an expired driver's license, credit card, and a picture of me...?

Wait, why does this guy have a picture of me? Unless...

I check his jacket. Keep the wallet, I thought. Oh, and sunglasses. In his jacket I find a pen, gun holster with an extra clip, and a small pale brown envelope marked with the initials G.A.

I know this shitty brown envelope, I've felt its grainy surface slide into my hand too many times, and I've never once enjoyed its texture, not once, not one bit. This envelope brings news, and it is never— and I mean never —good news.

This envelope is death.

I shoot up quickly, like I just got kicked where it counts. I feel like my stomach is in my throat. I turn towards the door, I feel fear. I feel afraid for the first time in a long time, viscous tough fear as thick if not thicker than molasses. I'm not quite yellow with fear, just far too uncomfortable with the thoughts running through my head.

After collecting the belongings of the recently departed, I think it best to leave before any authorities arrive. Though I'm not concerned with the police showing, I'm just not in the mood to explain what had happened. Self-defense, I was just defending what self I had left.

Into the main diner I proceed. Slowly and quietly, I collect myself. I make baby steps toward the exit. Patient, as my feet find their place. With every step, a bloodied footprint follows behind. The blood runs, seeping from my shoulder and with every step a terrible pain sears. I am wounded badly. I find myself stumbling to keep balance. I'm dazed by the gun shots, still sick with surprise. Unpleasant as that just was, at least I'm still standing. Well, trying to stand, that is.

Barren, the diner had been abandoned. The diner completely silent, besides my shoes that pleasantly stick to the floor soaked in my blood. The blood that runs from my shoulder wound down my chest, and right down my right leg on to the floor. I'm livid and stumbling for a booth. I'm observant despite my disarray and exhaustion.

For a moment I examine my surroundings. Know your exits, know their entries, and know where you're open for another attack. I quickly observe the area, with my hands directing my guns

in whichever direction I face.

That's when I notice the phone had been torn from the wall. The diner was probably abandoned right after the guns went off. Right before I went to take a piss, before someone walked in and unloaded two rounds in the stall I was in, hoping that the bullets fired killed me.

Suddenly, I feel a presence, someone else is nearby. I don't know how, but I know someone is nearby. Someone is hiding, breathing, and waiting to make a move. I shake the disorienting sickness that fights to overwhelm me. I feel my knees weaken, my stomach twist, and hot bile spills into my mouth.

A faint noise, that of a pin drop, echoes from behind me. Shaken, I turn quickly, my guns raised, indexes to triggers. Aim locked on a fat man with bottle cap glasses. A thick dirty beard, he's dressed in a white, dirty apron, and stinking of fear.

My unexpected action has stunned him. I realize suddenly that he could tear me to pieces with a spray from that shotgun he holds. But if he wanted to kill me in the first place, he would've pulled the trigger when I walked out of the washroom. We both stand absolutely still, guns familiarizing themselves, hearts pounding thunder.

"Don't you move, don't you fucking move!"

His tone coarse, as though he speaks through closed teeth, without etiquette, almost southern, it echoes in the emptiness of the diner, followed by a spray of spittle. His request is enforced by the gagging of a shell into its place. I stare, blinking.

This guy has balls, solid and brave.

A regular, or let me say, what appears to be a regular, diner chef is standing tall, gun pointed at a stranger who is heavily armed, unpleasant and bleeding in excess, recently victorious from the last dumb fuck who pointed a gun at him.

"Whoa. Listen buddy. Why don't we just put down the fire power and talk? How bout that? Because...honestly...I'm growing rather tired of having fucking guns pointed at me! "I bark at him, still standing, and with him in aim.

But a smile creeps over my face, innocent, lacking intent. My eyebrows peak as I motion my guns toward their hostlers. His gun slowly begins to descend, barrel towards the ground, but his eyes lock steadily on me, waiting for my next move. I just sigh with relief.

In a deep breath, his head hangs with his chin almost touching the top of his chest. His beard scratches the surface of his white apron, and then his gaze returns to me with a pleasant smile.

"Coffee?" he suggests casually, as an old friend would.

I nod and head towards the nearest booth. Sitting down, I turn my gaze to his direction. I patiently watch him rest his shotgun on the kitchen bar and grab a pot of coffee, lifting two ivory cups on his fingers and making his way to the booth. The cups clink together on his middle and ring fingers as he slowly approaches the booth I sit in.

Sliding in opposite to me, he lays down the cups and pot of fresh coffee. With an innocent smile, he pours two glasses and pushes one mug across to me.

"Have you called the cops yet?"

"No sir, shortly after you went into the bathroom, a man sitting right over there got up, cut the phone off the wall and before I could react, he pulled a gun and walked into the washroom."

He points to where my bathroom attacker had been waiting.

My eyes examine the place where he had been sitting when I walked into the washroom. He was sitting on the closest stool to the bathroom. But why didn't I recognize him when I walked in? I guess my attention surrounded the need to relieve myself before implosion.

I pull my cigarettes and Zippo from my jacket pocket, neatly placing them next to my coffee. I unbutton my new white shirt with my right hand while I stumble to get a cigarette out of the pack.

As my shirt opens, the chef's eyes begin to fix, his pupils grow, and his jaw drops. He isn't accustomed to seeing that much blood, at least not that much human blood.

"Sir you're hurt, hurt bad, we need to get you to a doctor," he insists frantically.

I shake my head in disagreement, resting a cigarette on my lips. His sincerity disturbs me. This guy cares, and not the hallmark concerned crap you see so often. He gives a shit. It's hard to find empathy, but he is natural. This is concern in a pure form.

I smile, letting the flame find the end.

Breathing in, I gaze at him steadily.

"What I do need is a medical kit, and something with ammonium hydroxide in it."

I slump back, exhaling.

He stares at me as if my eyes were crossed, or I just asked him the most uncomfortable thing. He sits there dumbfounded just gazing at me; suddenly, as if someone just slapped him, he nods and stands up.

"Yeah, Gordon the bus boy is training to be a paramedic; he keeps a medical kit in the back. But what is ammonium hydroxide?"

"Any type of industrial cleaner would do; do you have anything like that?"

He nods, stands up, and makes his way into the back behind the kitchen bar. I sit back staring at my coffee, my head is light and my vision blurs. Fuck, I've lost a lot of blood.

My shoulder is worse off than I thought, from the first slug; the second wound is a scratch, just a lucky flesh wound, but my right shoulder is throbbing. The gaping cavity hollows from my right shoulder and the blood runs like a fresh river in spring. As the snow melts, the water rushes, torrent and unforgiving. That's my wound, bleeding uncontrollably, and it appears to bleed without end.

I take another deep breath, moving my focus, changing my attention from the blood. I take my time observing the diner, because now, for the first time, I've got the peace and quiet I need.

The diner is classic. Black and white marble checkered tiles, red semi-circle booths embraced by steel tubing around the backs of them, salt, pepper, and small steel napkin dispensers on every table.

The big chef's voice interrupts my thoughts. "I got what you asked for."

He stands there before me proudly. In one hand a large nylon bag with a red cross on its face. In the other hand a jug of industrial cleaner, it sloshes as he places it on the table next to the medical bag. I take a moment to assess my situation, surroundings, and any thoughts before taking the jug from him.

I smile, as I reach for the jug of industrial cleaner; my eyes search its ingredients. Bingo. My smile widens, as I see printed clearly on the contents table: ammonia. I take my time slowly rising out of my seat. I try to hold myself up as I stand there bleeding out slowly. I'm lightheaded and tired but I have things to do, and I need to get them out of the way before I forget any minor details.

Every single last thing is relevant to my innocence and my disappearance. After I'm done cleaning this scene, I'm out. I'll have a coffee, a smoke, and then an open road. Nothing is going to stop me from leaving this dinner alive, no person, bullet, or unnatural occurrence will hinder my escape.

I need to know why and what the hell have I gotten myself into now. I'm used to trouble, but not like this, what the hell am I missing?

What time is it? My eyes search for the time, and I find it by listening for that constant ticking, over the washroom and slightly left of the door, the stained old clock presents the time, and I realize I've missed my medication. Fuck.

SECOND

Walking into the washroom I step over the corpse, smiling. In my hand a jug of ammonia, I approach the stall that was meant to be my grave. I begin to carefully examine the area for traces of my blood, presence, and being. On the wall above the toilet are two bullet holes, one encompassed by an eye of blood, and the other just a small hole, a couple feet away. The huge splatter effect is from the bullet that tore through my back and out of my right shoulder. All I remember is staring at the wall and then suddenly blood surrounding a smoking hole. I didn't even have time to put my dick away before the second bullet grazed my arm.

In that instance, I didn't freeze, I didn't scream, and I didn't flinch. I drew my M1911A1 cannon, turned, and began to fire as I dropped, spinning, to the floor. Little droplets of blood—my blood— stained the checkered bone white and onyx black tiles as I fell.

As I stand here now, examining the cross-firing pattern, I notice that these bullets tore through the stall door like it was paper, then burrowed deep into this badly painted wall. My bullets, likewise, tore back through the stall door and to my surprise had shattered all of the sink mirrors.

I dropped as I fired and all I heard was shattering glass. The deafening sound of thousands of falling pins. Glass shards had now overtaken this shitty pale floor.

Thunder for what felt like an eternity. I fell so slowly, I just let my finger do its work, pushing out round after round.

So many sounds echoed in this small washroom then, and as I think back to the cascading glass, the bullets and the blood, it's hard to discern what really happened. Or for that matter, in what order things occurred. But I'm alive and thankful that my retaliation gave me the distraction I needed to pull myself together.

Really though, how could I have predicted this? This was the last thing I would expect, someone trying to kill me while I was taking a leak and just trying to get my head around that, hurts. This guy walked into the washroom with the intention of killing me.

Who knew that I would turn that around, I'll bet he didn't. What's strange is that everything about this seems vaguely familiar. Not about shooting me in the stall, but how this guy walked in, without a care, and tried to kill me. Even worse, I know that this wasn't a random act of violence. It had been completely premeditated.

Which is strange, because I didn't even know I was coming here, so how the hell did he—or whoever hired him—know that I would be stopping at this diner?

Unless...

That would be fucking bad, and I don't mean crappy, I mean end-of-the-world for me kind of bad.

Because the only people that know, are the

people who sent me here, so why the hell would they try and kill me? It's hard trying to make sense of something that never made sense in the first place.

I roll my eyes and tip the jug, letting the ammonia splash out at my feet. Clear on crimson, cascading across the black and white tiles. The checkered design, aged with smoke and years of wear, kept the tiles a bone white. The red of my blood, the deep crimson, leaves a pink stain on the bone white as the ammonia moves across it. Filling the crevasses between the tiles and making its way around the floor, spreading ruby like the plague as it goes.

The stink fills my nostrils. Now instead of shit, I smell nothing but disinfectants, which, I guess, is a step up. The stench so potent I gag momentarily and before I vomit, I swallow it back down, wincing. I splash more on the bloody bullet holes in the wall.

Meticulously, I search for my biological traces. My blood. Watching the blood surrounding the bullet holes run down the wall, diluted with disinfectants. Entranced, I throw more chemical as if I was in a water fight. I intend to leave nothing dry.

I knew I had to do away with any evidence linking me to this place. I think I covered everything, except the chef. No, he's a nice guy. He lives. Johnny man, we don't go there, so stay off of it. I mean no offense by this, but he's a waste of bullets. Plus, he's the only friend I've got right now.

After wasting the entire jug of ammonia, I make my way back into the main diner from the washroom where I should've died; leaving it and its horrible stench for what I can only hope will be the last time.

Before leaving the washroom completely, I stop. I stand in the doorway and just witness the diner. I watch the glow of the sun between the multi-colored blinds across the dingy brown tables. I see it pierce through, uncaring, trying to reach everything it can, gleaming through half- empty glasses and full glasses, off plates and utensils. It ravages the diner with damp yellow light that dances in random patterns across the floor, it shines around the diner bouncing off the shiny metal fitted edges of the bar kitchen and off the glazed surfaces of my tired eyes.

I return to my pale table with my coffee, cigarettes, and the medical kit. I push the medical kit to the middle of the table and sigh, removing my black jacket, slowly one arm at a time, and I neatly lay it out on to the smooth table.

I sit still momentarily and just stare at this red and white medical kit. I'm lost and my mind is somewhere else.

The chef joyfully approaches holding a fresh pot of steaming coffee. He slides into the booth slowly across from me with a half-smile. The kind of smile you get from a concerned friend who hasn't seen you in a long time, with the sincerest intent of listening to the horror story that is your life.

Something familiar about his smile reminds me of home. Wherever that might once have been.

I push my empty mug towards him. I smile, with my head slowly turning to the left about to make a full circle to crack my neck, I just smile appreciatively. My fingers fold spider-like around the handle of the small mug, awaiting hot coffee to fill its emptiness with black warmth.

"I don't mean to get into your business sir, but is this a regular thing for you? I mean, do people usually go about shooting you in the john?"

The chef asks as politely as possible, given the question's nature.

I shake my head no vigorously with a large yellow smile, exhausting the little energy I have left, and fueling the one desire I have right now, sleep. But my little metal friend embedded in my shoulder advises me to keep my eyes open.

If someone is going to shoot me while I'm taking a leak, they sure as hell will have no problem doing the job while I'm sleeping.

Without honor, the lot of them, I guess it's kill or be killed, sadly. Until today, I didn't believe a word of that crap, in my opinion, it's "just don't get killed". But time changes opinions, I guess. Even mine.

I open the medical kit with a flick of my thumb. The top flies open and a smile creeps over my pale face. Inside, the items that may just save my life. Smile again.

Sterile gauze dressings, fabric knuckles, fabric adhesive, disposable gloves, ice packs, antiseptic wipes, scissors, tweezers, first aid guide, bandages, medical tape, and a hypodermic with enough Epinephrine for an overdose victim.

I slowly remove my shirt, God-damn, my shirt, the shirt that I bought less than several hours ago from a nearby department store. The once cloud- cotton white, collared, long sleeved dress shirt is now drenched in crimson from my overly enthusiastic wound. As the last button pops open, I notice the sponge that is my old under shirt, and now it has changed from the aged white of an over worn shirt to the red of my blood.

The wound in my shoulder is far worse than I assumed. From now on, completely fuck assumptions. Panic. I frantically shoot back the mug of black coffee; half of it goes down my throat, burning as it goes; the remainder on my face and shirt. Normally, that would've been quite painful, but right now I don't feel anything. It could be from the blood loss; it could be that I'm about to die, or hopefully it's just because I'm in shock.

Pray for shock because the first two have a bleak finality.

Fuck, Valentyne. Stay awake and I mean wide awake, do not blink, repeat words. I don't care. Just don't close your eyes or...

My mind screams.

I reach chaotically for the hypodermic of Epinephrine. I hold the safety tip in my mouth between my teeth and remove the cover on the needle with a tug. I've lost so much blood, even though earlier I could've sworn the wound wasn't as bad, but I guess I was shaken after getting shot. It must have grazed something, something too important to ignore. It must have cut an artery.

My mind now brutalized by thoughts of doubt, doubts of my existence after the diner and how much blood I'm losing. I'm fucking bleeding to death. Into the vein the needle goes, squeeze. Synthetic liquid enters my blood stream. The epinephrine begins a reaction and the adrenaline rush coming isn't my own. To think this small needle carrying such a small amount of this chemical could possibly have my heart beating as fast or faster than getting shot while taking a piss.

I can feel my heart pound, thumping painfully inside my rib cage, as if it will at any moment explode from my chest. Quickly, something inside changes, but it feels as if it may already be too late.

In this moment the chef is looking at me, while I'm looking at the needle that's buried in my arm, and nothing else, just the needle.

"Sir, how are you feeling? Cause you look really green, maybe I should call a doctor."

The chef asks with sincerity, like he knows me, like he cares.

As I sit here, propped up horribly, trying to keep my eyes open yet slowly fading from life, the chef's pleas for answer begin to become muffled, I blink unaware. I feel as if to die.

Darkness just behind me, it rises up from behind my eyes, absorbing my vision. I'm slipping from consciousness and slipping far too fast. I feel smothered as if wrapped in a wet blanket. I feel bound, restricted, limbs constricted; I feel crushed. I'm so tired.

Slowly, I feel like I'm slipping away, becoming content with these feelings. I relax like I'm in the midst of a tropical rainstorm and its downpour cools my skin from the burning sand beneath me.

I'm calm, visiting a place in my head. A pleasant memory, something saved.

An image locked away and saved for me and only me to find. Something from before today, before I can remember, something I just didn't know existed, I can feel my eyes open again, slowly, but they begin to open. When they do open, it's not the diner I see.

SOMETHING REMEMBERED

I'm in a creek, knee-deep in water. Cool, slow, sparkling calm water. My hair pulled back by my hands, which are interlocked behind my head. Here I am, staring up at clear azure sky with the sun shining, shining off the water and again reflecting from my eyes. The sound of water quietly sloshing around below and the soft chill of the summer breeze cuts around me, soothing my sweat-shined skin. I'm young again, tanned brown from being in the sun for too long, even though there is no such thing as too much time in the sun. Usually there just isn't enough time.

I'm younger here, the question is why here? Why this place? Everything here is so calm and cool. But I know I'm dying elsewhere. Here I'm relaxed and still as a statue. Calm and staring at the beautiful surroundings nature has provided me. I'm trapped in a virulent green maze with large oaks, tall pines and long grass. A panoply of insects that call it home. At some point, so did I.

The silence breaks, my calm destroyed. A forgotten memory returns and with it, I now know what this place is. But why am I choosing now to remember this place, of all places? This memory now, repressed like so many others, floods back uncontrollably, and I'm reminded.

I haven't moved, as if I'm frozen, unflinching standing in the stillness of the creek. The sun burning down from above and I'm motionless with my hands on my head, my eyes jetting left to right, my fingers intertwined beneath my muddy hair, and my teeth grind mechanically left to right.

Wait.

Why are my hands on my head?

My torn jeans hang low on my waist accompanied by my favorite leather belt. Lonely on my belt is a knife sheath, my knife, oh shit this is...

This must be where I lost my knife.

The knife sheath empty and missing the beautifully ornate dagger that once filled its volume, a finely crafted seven-inch blade with a razor edge, a clean, straight handle, an eagle's head on the pommel.

This must be the day I lost it, but something is wrong with this place. I don't mean about losing my knife, something just doesn't fit; something makes me unfathomably uneasy. That feeling should be foreign here, because everything about this place is just the opposite—it is easy—so now I'm not.

It's peaceful here, how the sun streams through the treetops, cutting across the surface of the calm creek, mirrored and dancing from each side of the creek bed, gleaming brightly as noon makes day. But I can see it in my face, because right now, I know I don't want to be here. Standing in the middle of the creek up to my knees, my hands locked behind my head.

Something bad, something unbelievably terrible is about to happen. So, I wait, and I watch. In my mind one sentence keeps repeating. It was an accident. It was a fucking accident. I didn't mean to.

My lips move but no sound comes from them. I'm yelling back at someone. Someone is behind me, but I still don't turn. I think I know what's going on, but I don't think I want to remember what happens next.

In an instant, the silence disperses, I can hear noise, but not from my voice. It's the person's voice, the person I'm replying to, the person behind me, screaming at me, screaming for me to turn around, screaming at me just like when you're yelling at a child for behaving inexcusably.

I'm that child.

Now my hands, like a clock, click down in front of my face, between the cracking mud, I see blood...

Oh, fuck me, what've I done?

Scanning, I search around for my answers. I find them floating in the water in front of me, right fucking in front of me, bobbing like an apple in a barrel, my answers came right before this moment, and they came with a killing blow.

No.

No, I couldn't have killed. Why would have I killed someone, anyone, back then? But there in front of my half-naked, twenty-year-old self is a buoyant, drenched, and almost completely submerged corpse, with my knife now lodged deeply in his lumbar. Only the corpses back erects from the water's surface, the pommel of my knife desperately tries to stay surfaced as if it's trying not to drown. Helplessly, it begins to sink.

I hear the voice again telling me to turn around. I feel the cold sweat bead from every exposed pore and the unexposed areas, suffocating. I feel targeted, helpless, and trapped. I'm at the mercy of an unwanted memory and there, behind me to my left is a stranger. To make things worse, he's the bad kind of stranger. He's the kind with a gun.

The gun is pointed at me, I don't know who this gun-wielding maniac is, but he sounds like a cop. He's shouting at me, trying to convince me to turn around slowly and face him. But I just calmly stare down at my kill, ignoring his orders; I'm focused on my hands.

The hands I no longer know. These tools capable of creation are now simply killing instruments. These hands are my own.

These hands have their own personality covered in blood, the blood of my recent victim, and all I can do is stare, disappointed in them.

Finally, I spin around and face this stranger. He stands solid, gun raised, hot with frustration. His voice rasps without concern, he begins to talk instead of scream, but the anger is still there, seeping through clenched teeth. He's right about to scream again, but he manages to keep his voice down despite the fury that urges him to pull the trigger. The last thing you want to be doing in that state is holding a gun, no matter who you are.

We lock eyes, mine dark and empty, staring right back into his eyes, his irises absent, surround by crimson roots, his sockets engulfed by terrible throbbing veins. Muscles pull his eyes to a squint as they burn back into my stare. He's haunted by anticipation, my next move unknown. The gun has not moved from its solidified target. That target is my head. As he catches his breath,

I can now hear what he says, as clear as the crystal surface of this still creek.

"Get on your knees son and do it quick. Get those hands back on your head, turn and sink— and understand this. If you move, you are fucking dead. Dead. Do you comprehend dead? I don't want an answer, just do what I said."

He shouts, collapsing the tone of his once-calm voice, flailing the gun, making a show of it, trying to scare me, trying to shake me. Yet, I continue to stare at him. I'll let you in on something. I've never been able to deal with authority, especially when it is

screaming at me to do something I don't want to do, and furthermore when it's pointing a gun at me.

And that's when I pick up on it.

Why is he shaking?

Bile rises in my throat; something is extremely wrong here. I'm unable to follow; it's like walking into the middle of a movie and trying to follow the plot. You know at this point there is nothing to do here but watch from that point on, so you do anyways, because you paid for the ticket. Ok so maybe it's not exactly the same; you can always get a refund. There are no refunds here. Just sit there, sit and watch.

Now my thoughts sway in a direction I wish not to go in. Even in this memory, I fight this choice. This and everything around me is surreal, all with a hint of error. Everything inside me screams for me to run. My blood boils for a reaction but rationality is convincing. He has a gun aimed at my skull; with my luck, he knows how to use it.

I slowly begin to sink into the cool water below and as I do, it floods into my pockets. Soothing its way to my waist as I start to turn my back to him, the water's mild chill wakes me. My breaths heavy and separate as I finish turning, giving him my back, my hands are once again interlocked behind my muddy wet hair. The blood again runs—not from a wound but from my fingers—and melts into my hair.

Behind me, I can hear him step into the water. He swears loudly as he stumbles, a splash followed by mumbled obscenities. Loud, echoed sloshing sounds as he makes his way towards me. He's getting close, and I'm running out of time to act.

The silence begins to consume me again.

Everything is quiet but my breathing and the sounds of the water. Deeply I inhale, slow and rhythmic, sucking air deep inside my unforgiving lungs. I can hear the water separate and rejoin itself as he gets closer, closer, closer.

I can now see his reflection in the water. A normal reflection at first, but as he gets closer, the ripples destroy the once-human image, altering it into some kind of distorted illusion. Simultaneously, our two images become one and then I see the truth staring right back at me. This man isn't a cop. He isn't a friend or someone I know, like, or dislike.

Thank God for small town syndrome. If I hadn't been paying attention, if I had given in to his demands, if I hadn't suspected anything, then I wouldn't have noticed that this man doesn't reach for his cuffs, because he doesn't have any fucking cuffs. He pulls back the hammer on his gun.

In front of me, the corpse floats, bobbing. Behind me, the stranger stands unfriendly, ready and willing to pull the trigger at any moment. Now my mind screams. It's not fear, anticipation or question. It's react. Just react, react now, react right fucking now, Johnny.

A deep breath as I dig my toes into the mud, I feel my heartbeat thunder.

My enemy is directly behind me, the barrel of his gun about to touch the back of my head. A smile creeps across my face.

I react. In one fluent motion, I tear my knife from the corpse, kick myself backwards hard, knocking him down. My unsuspecting adversary is not prepared to take a blow to the chin. The back of my head catches his narrow chin hard, and the force of my attack sends us both back into the shallow water below.

I dig my legs into the soft mud and use my body as an anchor. I can feel him struggling beneath me in the murky darkness of the stirred-up water. I spin around and plant my knees on his chest, quickly lifting my upper body out of the water. I begin to systematically thrust my arm down hard, stabbing at him blindly. Suddenly, a flash of light, something hits me hard in the side of the head.

I crash to the right and sink into the creek from the gun butt to my skull. I lay still, absolutely still, sinking down. I feel fresh blood inking from a wound. From the opaque darkness, I see my opponent's legs, and he's again standing. I can barely make out his pant legs, but I know where he is.

He slowly turns around in the same spot like a carousel but he's jerking left to right. He's lost me in the water. The mud that got kicked up from our struggle provides excellent cover.

Swimming to the left of him, I take my place. He once again stations himself in the muddy creek bed, examining the water. I put my left hand and both feet into the creek bed, preparing to leap predator-like; I'm running out of time and air as I feel my lungs bursting.

I've been under for far too long, but I don't want to chance any mistake in this attack, my coup-de-grace. My attack can and will end the chaos. Lung's bursting, I tear out of the crystalline prison. Water rains down around me as my body cuts into the air. My enemy's eyes widen as he spins to face me. He raises his arm that holds the gun, my real enemy, but his actions are entirely futile, as quick as he may be, it's already too late. My right arm comes down with the collective kinetic force of my entire body, my knife shreds through his solar plexus, and I release my dead-lock grip of the hilt. This all happens before my feet even reach the creek bed. I slump down, my hands touching the water, with my back arched towards the sky.

His eyes begin to squint, and he lets out a muffled groan that's quickly silenced as blood pours from between his grinding teeth. Almost getting out a word,

"Fuck."

He begins to fall, toppling like a downed tree, his eyes roll back into his head. My eyes follow his slow descent into the unforgiving water. I begin to rise slowly, watching him grab the hilt of the knife, with his free hand, intent on removing it. His right hand rises towards me. His right hand is the hand that holds the gun.

Flash, one round is squeezed out. I flinch as I feel the bullet fly by me. A second shot is followed by more uncontrollable flinching. My heart pounds from another miss. His gun goes off again two more times.

Miss.

And then hit.

I feel blood trickle down from a wound at my hairline, dead center on the top of my skull, right where the hair would part if I parted my hair at all. The stream of blood slowly drips down my nose, onto my dry cracked lips, and rolls onto my bare chest.

I hear a splash as he hits the water and finally begins to sink. I look down as the water reclaims the space where he once stood.

Dizziness. I'm lightheaded, a stream of blood continuously running off the tip of my nose onto my bottom lip, bouncing like a waterfall over rocks. My balance begins to alter, I begin to stagger and then slip as my legs lose strength. My heart continues to beat furiously and then the beat sounds and feels as if doubled, not in speed but signature. I can hear my heart beating twice over.

Helpless, I fall backwards, and when my back touches the surface of the creek water, all I feel is cold. A burst of awareness as I fall. It feels as if the water reaches up to catch my fall. To lovingly cradle to my form, like a mother with her child. Slowly the water wipes away the dryness. Every inch of my body slowly conforms to the center from back to front. My pupils grow larger as I slowly sink. I watch the blazing sun, the azure sky, and the cotton clouds above me.

The calming sounds of this tranquil creek lulling me away; without warning, water fills my ears, deaf. The sun distorts, the clouds blur, and the blue of the sky turns grey. The last image I see, the sun, explodes above me and light overtakes the sky, followed quickly by darkness, taking its place among the heavens. The last part of my body slowly begins to be consumed by the water.

The water quickly fills my nostrils, and I've become incoherent. As the dark slowly comes, a different sensation deeply fills me, swallows me whole. Then, the bounding echo of a voice, my voice, crying out to me.

"Hold on."

The water forms over my sockets. Blinking, it blurs my vision. I cannot form thoughts, sinking, this flaccid transparency is far too pleasant, and this creek is vindictively pure.

My back softly touches the creek bed; I feel cold and slightly scared. I open my mouth to take in water, ready to die here even though I know I didn't.

The diner, what about the diner?

I feel pressure as someone tugs me up through the surface of water. My head breaks the surface, and I gasp deeply for air. But I can't see anything. No diner and no creek.

A complete and total emptiness, diverted from reality, except for the occasional dull burst of pain.

I've started to consider the possibility of death here, but I'm alive elsewhere. In this moment, right now, I'm sitting, prone, defenseless, unconscious, but alive.

I can't make out anything comprehensible, nothing visual or mental. No images or memories. Why can't I fucking remember anything? What scares me most is that I can't motivate myself to wake up. There is only the attempt to remember something, anything. I just want to feel.

The pain penetrates me again, wave after wave now. It's a cold sweat, a sick, bowel-wrenching kind of pain. My heart grows tighter, as if someone has their hand on it. I'm sick and trying desperately to come back to reality.

My mind flashes other short glimpses of memories that are purely visual. The only sound I hear is humming, maybe a buzz. The sound you receive when you smack a tuning fork against glass and hold it close to your ear.

I see the creek again but this time it's from above, a bird's eye view, as if I'm flying.

Flash, then darkness returns, and I'm blinded once again. Then, sunlight. Golden sunlight barrages my lids. Opening them slightly, I can see the stained ugly tables of the diner. They're blurry but they're there. Full images slowly appear as my sight clears away the fog.

Blink, and blink again. Am I conscious?

I don't think so.

Without warning, I fall back into the darkness, and then I open my eyes to the creek and its beautiful sky above. But this time, somehow, I'm looking down at myself from someone else's eyes.

"What the fuck?"

I hear my voice inside my head scream, and then these eyes look at the water. The water is still, except the two bobbing corpses, the one who had my knife and the one who is now impaled by it.

But I'm not in the water. I lose this image as if the person has shut their eyes closed; I can hear something being whispered in my ear. I can't decipher the whispers because something else is drowning the sound out.

Blinded by light as my eyes open, I see sun and shadows. The sky above spins and I've been pulled from the creek. Someone kneels beside me and I can't tell if they are friend or foe. The blood running from the wound on my head colors the sky blue to crimson and I can feel grass at my back and crusted mud all over my body and clothes.

The figure reaches down and gently caresses my face, soothing fingers sliding from my forehead to my lips, brushing over my cheeks. The fingers fold under my chin, providing support, so I can raise my face and look up.

I cannot make out who the person is, but their grace suggests someone female. She cradles me in her arms and warms me with her embrace. I can feel the crusted mud soften and crack off my face. I feel water drop on my lips and my dried tongue licks it from their chapped surface.

I taste something, and then I know what it is. The taste is salt; the taste is tears.

I close my eyes, feeling sick from trying to make out images around me. Suddenly I can hear a beat, calm and simple. It's soft, caring, thumping with fear. The beat begins to grow louder, with every second comes thunder, and after a minute, the beat is all I can hear. Her heart is all I can hear. She holds on tight, on the shore of this tranquil creek, lying under a tree amongst soft long grass. This girl, this beautiful girl, has dragged me to safety, out of sight, and fight.

Sadly, I'm stolen from this memory. This peaceful memory, a memory I need to remember. If I am to find out about my past, I should take some time to figure out what happened here, why I lost it, why would I lose something like this, something so happy.

Out of my thoughts like a shot in the dark I return from just before I got shot.

It is as if my memories are rewinding, trying to show me something.

What am I looking for?

Freeze to the image of the barrel, the barrel from my attacker.

Watching the last bullet tear from the gun, as the round leaves the chamber separating from its casing before traveling down and out the barrel.

Focusing on me, avoiding the path of the last bullet, the bullet meant to kill, the bullet that tore the top of my skull, but the bullet from his gun, the last bullet, it misses me.

Wait, then how did I get this head wound?

Almost instantaneously, another one explodes like a round in my thoughts; a gun goes off elsewhere. Someone else's gun goes off. Someone just behind him, just behind my attacker, on his direct left, a figure shrouded in shade.

I feel the bullet slowly shredding my scalp as it lodges itself in the crown of my skull. As I fall backwards into the water, I see the shooter.

Standing under the tree is a beautiful young woman; her chocolate brown hair pulled back, her face stained with instantaneous regret, her mouth gaping in awe as she sees the victim of her shot. Her hand releases the smoking pistol.

She wasn't aiming at me.

I watch the tears well in her eyes as I fall, and slowly her lips part for a word, but she moves instead. I watch her take flight from the spot where she stands, into the creek, toward me.

THIRD

Confusion as my eyes rip open and my reflexes are suddenly and surprisingly sharp. I'm flooded with questions, emotions, and strength. I'm back at the diner and out of my seat, leaning fully forward with my guns conveniently placed under the chef's chin. My teeth grind painfully left to right.

My breathing is painfully erratic, desperately I try to slow it, realizing what I'm doing, where I am, I've regained consciousness and I'm awake.

The poor chef's eyes are wide, and he's frozen with his hands above his head. His arms shake and his lips quiver. My fingers locked on the triggers of my guns, accurately positioned for a squeeze, and if I just pull my fingers at all toward me – the chef's dead.

Heavy beads of sweat roll down my forehead. My shoulders slump in the sad attempt to relax, I begin to slide backwards to where I was originally
sitting, removing the barrels and releasing the hammers.

Sighing, I make a sorry attempt to sincerely smile. "Sorry."

The chef comfortably slumps back in his seat, soaked with relief.

"How long have I been unconscious?"

The chef's eyes begin to relax behind those large bottle cap glass lenses barely held to his face by a simple crooked frame.

"It hasn't been that long sir – your jacket was ringing."

The chef sits up and pushes my jacket toward me. It's beeping—my jacket—is beeping.

I reach for my dirty black coat, all the while my guns still locked in my hands. My crippled fingers push from the triggers. My hands stiff, refusing to release my metallic guardians from what would be their grave.

Put the guns down and pick up the jacket, Johnny. It's the best idea, considering I really need to relax. My current injury is oxygen—I lack oxygen.

I remind myself.

Oxygen, breathe in as if I'd just erupted from that mirrored prison, the creek. Jumping back into my skin and trying to come to terms with this situation is increasingly difficult. What that was and why I didn't remember it until now.

Let my wound clot, let the blood build in the vein, and slowly scab scarlet. Everything, absolutely everything around me feels dull, still, and dying with the fine exception of the chef.

But my thoughts are on my phone, the phone that hides deep within my jacket pocket. I don't want to answer the phone, not after today, and not anymore.

I'm divided. I don't want to know but I can't help myself from opening the phone and dialing my voice mail via number one. My hand shakes as I press the phone close to my ear, the robotic voice of my mailbox asks for the password, and she receives it.

Impatiently, I listen. Press one to listen to previously heard, press two to reply, press three to hear new messages. Pressing three leads me to another option, press one again to hear message now—it's marked urgent. Press one to listen now. I just want to listen to my messages—in this one and only scenario, I don't need these many options.

The chef sits silently, his brows raised, and he waits patiently for me to tell him the news.

Who was this mystery message from? Did it have anything to do with this?

The chef sits up, with a smile, shallowly breathing in with his fat nostrils trying to be as quiet as possible but it's not working.

Message –

"Valentyne, I wish you could've been a tad more professional in resigning your position. However, I understand your need to pursue other career options, and we will surely miss you."

Dial tone –

Light the fire of fear and let it burn eternally. I now see it; this could be my end. Nothing could retract this delusion, a delusion which became my reality only moments ago.

This is where I live or die, bleeding in this diner, slipping in and out of consciousness.

My life could suddenly be stolen at any moment; that thought is no more a thought, it's infallible knowing, the next possibility. I don't know what to do, what's the plan? Think Johnny.

As one man I'm powerless and as this sets in, I feel sick. I want to evacuate the contents of my stomach on to this pale floor below my feet. One word repeats like a whisper in my ear – disappear, disappear. Something inside me falsifies that desire, for some reason, I don't want to run. Even though it seems like the most logical approach. Logically, running would at least offer my life longevity.

I battle for control, control over my thoughts, physical consciousness, and control over what to do next. What to do? In this moment it appears— out of all those many things—I can control none for the moment.

For moments, what I wouldn't give for more moments. Enough time to look around and just enjoy what could be my last day here. It's disturbing how mortality comes when you're actually staring death in the eyes, and you've just changed your mind. He's not happy and he's not going to give you up without one hell of a fight.

My guns are running empty. I can barely keep my eyes open. I have no idea what's coming and my only known ally is the chef. I look at him and all he does is politely nod, filling my cup of coffee, patiently awaiting my next action.

He's about as uncomfortable or more than I am except he's trying to hide it.

Distracting myself from these overwhelming fears, I look to my shoulder wound and it has stopped bleeding. I'm still in dire need of medical attention. It could be worse, but it's not.

Smiling, I slowly slide my guns down perpendicular to my coffee cup, symmetrically across from each other, leaving just the cup separating them.

Reaching into my jacket, I remove my crushed pack of nameless cigarettes. Carefully, I remove two from the pack and with a flick I toss one between my lips, and hand the chef the other. Removing my Zippo, I sit up, taking my posture back. Flick, the lid opens followed by the awakening scent of fresh lighter fluid. The smell calms me as my thumb turns the steel abrasively against the flint; within seconds the sparks light the blackened wick, and I have fire.

I sigh, take a long deep breath inwards and sink back into the booth. I let the thick opaque smoke slowly escape from between my lips as my head finds rest against the padded red leather that covers the booth.

Sitting in silence, the chef and I stare. Enjoying the silence, I explore the storm of my mind.

This situation couldn't get any worse, but I manage to stay calm.

Let go of the stress, let go of this twisted situation, and just figure out what to do. Clueless, I chuckle under my breath. Collecting the few scattered scenes of my memory, I inhale again deeply. As I exhale my focus goes to the scenery outside.

Peering through the shades, the soft orange light from the sun pours in. I open the blinds with my index finger and the sunlight peacefully spills in and blankets the diner. The light makes its way over and across tables, pushing the darkness into the corners, out and off the floor, reflecting through half-filled glasses of water and soda. A prismatic dance as dusk takes day. I slowly let go, just concentrating on this beautiful sight. The orange glow and the shadows mix, picture perfect. Exhaling, I watch the bone-white smoke tint blue as if the clouds came down from the sky. This is how night washes away the day, tranquilly, blissfully, smothered by deceptive comfort.

This is how my "vacation" should've begun, but this isn't a vacation.

Right now, it sure could be, but not in the hours prior.

Horror, beauty, and death all in the same day followed closely by a lingering fear of the night ahead. I consider what to do, embrace the natural change or fight it. Dusk has fallen. Going over the recent events I ponder my next step. Get lost and never be found seems like the most logical option but that doesn't work for me. I've never been good at lying low nor do I like doing it. So, my only option is to figure out what the hell happened.

Strangely, the chef sits quietly this entire time as if nothing had happened or this was the most exciting thing he had ever seen. As if this was a blessing, a long-desired break to full-time honest work. Damn it, how I envy the simple life—but the problems of a simple life are sometimes too great, especially on minimum wage.

He sits back and stares out the window enjoying the cigarette I gave to him. I breathe and

he's still. Comfort to my discomfort, and I guess it's proper.

I'm sitting up staring at this poor bastard. Mumbling away, mumbling about the shirt. What the fuck is so important about this shirt?

Let's go over its history: besides being brand new, where I bought it. Here in this stain of a town nothing really special comes to mind—I mean, it looks good on me—wait, does it? Have I even looked? No, no, I haven't looked.

Well, this is where I start wondering and mumbling louder.

"What?"

The chef sits up, staring back at me, popping a sincere half-smile when he occasionally feels comfortable enough, but my stare has been unbroken and I'm just looking at him—maybe not directly, because I may as well be able to see right through him, just because my eyes are directly on him and they don't even blink – oh, yeah –

"Sorry, I'm just thinking out loud."

Doesn't mean I want anything. I don't feel like talking to anyone but myself.

"What are you thinking about?" "The way I look."

"What does that have to do with anything that's going on sir? Or does it? I'm sorry, I shouldn't intrude, your business is yours. Am I a hostage or something?"

"No, hey, if you want to leave you can go." "Well...not exactly, friend. This is my diner
and I'm not going anywhere."

"Oh shit, I didn't mean it like, fuck, I'm sorry about all of this."

"It's not your fault; anyhow, the insurance will cover the damage. You're the one with people trying to kill you. I'm sorry to ask but I have to know, what's that all about?"

"Honestly?" "Huh?"

"Have an hour?" "Yeah, but do you?"

"That's a good point."

I realize I can't chat. I have to get the fuck out of this diner before any more of the company comes. I'm screwed if I stay. Then it dawns on me like day. I came for a reason, this place called out to me, and I don't think it's just because of hunger, the need to relieve myself, or that I felt like stopping in for a coffee—I felt drawn to it, like these memories. Since I bought that shirt, something happened to me. Everything was grey or black upstairs, never thinking, always moving, and never remembering anything other than the task at hand.

Now as I'm about to leave, half-standing, still half-sitting, I can't even remember what that task was. My head starts to pound methodically, and I realize I need to take my medication.

With that thought, my hand robotically goes to my pocket, and I pull forth a small orange plastic vial with a white sticker littered with grey writing which reads like Latin.

The chef looks at me, looks at the pills, and then back to me with what looks like the intent to form a sentence, but he stores it with silence as he looks back to his half-empty mug. I look down at him, I'm still in a sit-going-to-stand position, and then my legs give out and suddenly I'm back in my seat.

As I land, I look at the chef who throws me a big warm smile and shakes the semi full coffee pot. With my thumb and index, I free the lid from the pill bottle. I dump two black and grey pills into my hand. I cock my hand back with the intent to throw these little marked pills down my throat and the chef returns with a sentence.

"What are those?" "My medication." "What for?"

"For the chemicals I lack." "Which chemicals are those?"

"Something to do with the parts of my brain I lost to a bullet."

"What?"

"Well, I lost certain key grey matter that produces chemicals needed for long term memory organization."

"Memory organization? Like amnesia? I've never heard of memory organization."

"It's like amnesia, except I remember some things, but they aren't in the correct order—at least—what I do remember isn't in the right order. The only similarity between my condition and amnesia is there are things I've completely forgotten."

Like a child he stares, mystified by my condition, not just interested but fully consumed by my injury.

"Yeah, I took a bullet here."

I pull my hair back to expose my scar, a scar from a bullet, a bullet from a gun, a gun from someone I can't remember. My mind revolves around one sentence...

It was an accident.

My hand starts to ascend to my face, the pills prepare to be ingested, and I prepare to relax, but my eyes still focus on the chef and what he says makes me stop this ritual.

"Well, do they work? I mean, do they help you remember?"

That sentence seemed to come on as gibberish but in his innocence he's right.

Do they work?

"You know, it may sound idiotic, but... I don't know. I'm starting to think I'm better off without them."

"Then why the hell would you take them?"

After every sentence I begin to wonder how strange this is. The only time I remember anything about my past is when I forget to take my pills— how odd, and yet so idiotic of me.

What the fuck is wrong with me? How is that not obvious?

My hand starts to shake, as something inside is forcing me to take them, and I can't stop myself.

In my head I can hear whispering, instructive whispering, and the sickness begins. There in the palm of my hand, subconsciously, without my own desire, I try to believe this is the medicine for my sickness, but now, now I know there is something horribly wrong with me, and with these drugs because I'm at war with indecision.

A part of me knows they won't help, that part of me is sure of it, but something inside continues to attempt to falsify that, to convince that they will.

"Sir?"

My hand seems to be forced closer, inch by inch, slowly pushed forward but I desperately hold it back. I'm shaking, mumbling, and disoriented.

I fight the feeling, the need, and the desire to take these little grey and black bastards.

What do those colors represent? Wait, what?

What does the colors of these pills have to do with anything?

My eyes close and it begins anew, another flooding memory, but this time is the first time I've seen it, any of it.

When I open my eyes, I'm sitting up in a hospital gown, and right across from me is another man in the exact same hospital gown. Sitting on the same chair, sitting exactly how I'm sitting, staring at me exactly as I'm staring at him. We're the same height, the same build, same hair color, and his eyes are exactly like mine—deep brown, almost cherry.

"Valentyne, how do you feel?"

He says with a strange adjusting smile, as if this is the first time he has smiled.

"I feel like I got hit by a truck, my head is pounding, and I'm dizzy but other than that I'm peachy thanks. Now, who and how the fuck are you?"

He smiles, blinks several times, then chuckles. "In a good mood now and I'm sorry for not

previously introducing myself. I'm Greyor.

I cut in sharply without regard for his next words.

"Greyor? What kind of fucking name is Greyor? Is that your last name?"

He shakes his head.

"My full name is Greyor Allblack."

"Is that seriously your name, cause if you wanted to make something up, I'd reconsider."

His eyes stop naturally moving, they solidly lock into my stare, and this is the first time I've ever looked away from someone after offending them. This guy scares me, and all he did was look at me. It's something behind his eyes that makes my skin crawl, he has intimidated me by just looking at me, and I'm now speechless.

Nothing calm or comfortable can be said and I try desperately to remedy this, but I can't speak, so I just look down.

"Listen man, I didn't mean anything, I'm just surprised is all, it's a cool name man."

"Thank you, Johnny."

The cold leaves as a warm smile creeps over his face, not comforting, but better than that cadaverous stare.

"Ok Greyor, where the hell am I?" "A hospital."

"What hospital?"

The eyes return and his smile disappears but this time, this time I don't look away, I lock eyes without a blink and with this stare I'm haunted by familiarities.

"If I told you Johnny, you wouldn't remember it anyways."

"Well, try me." "Southstone."

"Nope, you're right, nothing." "See?"

"What happened?"

"You have brain damage, friend." "When did that happen?"

I smile, trying to hide the fact that I'm afraid, smothering fear with sarcastic curiosity.

"A bullet tore through the top of your skull, cleverly trimming necessary grey matter, and now you won't be able to remember anything prior to the surgery."

Denial fills me whole; I stammer at first, and then shake my head in disbelief, but at this point in time, he's right, I can't remember anything except the pale teal walls of this hospital.

"Don't bother. It's going to hurt more than help."

"What will?"

"Remembering. Johnny, you're responsible for the deaths of six people, and the only reason that you're not in an eight by ten cell is that you've got severe brain damage, and the judge deemed you incapable of mental responsibility. So, you've been sentenced to serve it here at Southstone, until we deem you corrected, and capable of societal re- entry, without any relapses."

"Wow, ignorance really is bliss, isn't it?"

At this point in time, in my timeline, I guess I

I really didn't remember, or maybe it's because I couldn't remember.

"Yes Johnny, I guess it is, anyhow we need to get you rested for your rehabilitation."

He says calmly, smiling.

"Rehabilitation? What do you have in store for me?"

"Antipsychotic medication trials, full physiotherapy, and cognitive re-education."

"Will I ever remember anything?"

"Maybe, it's hard to say; maybe you'll remember something or maybe nothing...at...all."

"Why did you just take your time finishing that?"

"Finishing what?" "Your sentence."

"Oh, nothing at all? Well, Johnny, that's a story for a different day, ok?"

He nods at me, and as soon as his eyes leave mine, he looks elsewhere, and my eyes close.

Yet another memory I may have to wait to understand because the next time I open my eyes; I'm looking at the chef.

FOUR

"Welcome back friend, I thought I lost you again."
"What'd I miss?"

"Nothing really, except you dropped your pills on the floor. I was going to pick them up, but I didn't really want to disturb you, cause the last time I tried, you reacted rather violently."

"Wise move my friend, wise move. Hey, do you want a smoke?"

Inside my left ear I hear ringing, not from a phone, and not of a tuning fork, it sounds at first like beeping and begins to sound less mechanical and more than that of a whisper, a pulse, a complete auditory hallucination.

"Do you hear that?" "Hear what?"

Ok, it's confirmed, I'm hallucinating.

I focus to make out the whispers, to hear what they say, the chef says something, but now this voice drowns him out and I can't hear what he says. The voice repeats one sentence, over, and over. The sentence is initials.

The voice repeats three letters over and over:

"J. R. V... J.R.V." and then the voice gets quieter.

I shake my head and with it the voice. It dissipates the more I focus on my cigarettes, the more I concentrate on the chef. The more I do, the less I hear it, and when the chef speaks again, like a light being turned off, it's gone.

"Sir, do you mind if I enquire about something?"

"Shoot."

He giggles under his shaggy beard; he looks at me strangely as if I just said something adorable, and then again begins to speak.

"What does that tattoo stand for?"

His chubby hand points toward my chest right near my left shoulder, just before the armpit becomes chest. I have the letters JRV tattooed in Old English calligraphy.

I freeze, staring at this tattoo, never seeing it till now, completely unaware of its existence.

I now immediately know what these initials stand for, but I just don't understand why it means what it means.

"Just remember violence." "Well, what does that mean?" "I don't know."

"Well why would you have it tattooed on you?" "Don't know that either."

"Sir, you're starting to remind me of someone."

His eyes seem to glisten temporarily, his cheeks shake, and he seems as if he's about to cry. But he stops himself and sucks in a deep breath of air and pulls off a smile.

"Now, about that cigarette?"

I smile and extend the brown dotted filter of a poking cigarette, he takes it and nods, he slides back and stares out the blinds. He reaches for a lighter stuffed somewhere behind his apron and draws the fresh flame to the end drawing in a massive breath, he then blows a portion of the smoke from his nose and goes quiet.

"The man who came in here, who cleared the diner, that same guy who attempted to kill me in the washroom, well, we used to work together."

The chef slowly turns his head to look at me, his face begins to go white, and he's shocked at my choice of conversation starters.

"What the hell do you do? I mean, what kind of work ends up turning into a shootout? What did you do, get his promotion or something?"

I giggle and shake my head.

"No, I think...it is because I failed to do my job."

"What the hell didn't you do?"

"I didn't kill the person I was sent here to kill." "You kill people, for a living? I mean that's

kind of backwards. No offense." "None taken."

"Why?" "Insurance." "Insurance?"

"I kill people for a criminal organization that poses as a life insurance company."

His eyes wide, jaw dropped, he's solidly petrified by what I'm saying. He looks unconvinced almost like he thinks I'm lying.

"How does that work, I mean, you just can't kill people and get away with it."

"You ever hear of black-market organ dealing?" He just stares at me.

"Basically, someone dies, so someone else can live, in some cases, the people dying have a choice, and sadly in other cases they don't. But in the end, someone gets to live. Well, the people I work for—as sick as it sounds—have the same philosophy."

He still doesn't understand, but then again, neither do I.

"You see, the people I work for, or should I say used to work for, hand pick individuals, offer them a seemingly innocent insurance policy, and once accepted they've just signed their life away, yes, the family gets compensated, but so does the company, they're making fucking millions off these deaths, and I enforce these policies, I carry them out.

I don't know how they get away with it, but they do. I guess death isn't so hard to deal with if the results drastically change your situation. People are just blinded by dollars."

"That's horrible, you can't put a price on life.
No amount of money is worth that."

"Well, sadly, they do, and that price has several zeroes involved."

"How'd you get into this line of work and why in god's name would you want to?"

"They recruited me during my recovery. To be honest, I didn't have a problem with it, until I got here, something about this town, woke me up."

"What do you mean woke you up?" "This shirt."
"Your shirt?"

"She said it looked good on me." "Who did?"

"The girl at the department store." "Which department store?"

"The only one, ha."

I hold my laughter because the chef's face sours at my last comment.

"Cheyenne, you know it?"

"Yes sir. Did this girl have beautiful eyes, dark hair, and the most gorgeous smile you've ever seen?"

I smile, and nod.

"Her eyes were color in color, the single most beautiful sight I have ever seen."

"That's Jess. She's a great girl, never been the same since"

He pauses,

"Hell, you don't need to hear about that. Damn, you sure do remind me of him though, you even talk like him."

"Him?"

"Her Johnny. She was never the same after he died. To my knowledge she never moved on.

She never even looked at another man, until you, apparently."

"What happened to Johnny?"

"Well, he fell into trouble a while back, got himself killed. Jess and his two best friends wouldn't drop it, they always said he wasn't dead. It was sad how they kept all his stuff, his car, his clothes, even his guitar. They never let him go. Hell, he's dead, I went to the funeral, I saw them bury his coffin, and I watched them place his head stone. Those three never let up, kept saying he was alive."

"Why would they say that? Didn't they see his coffin buried?"

"Yeah, they were there, most of the town was there, but his funeral was closed casket, which is odd because it wasn't much of a wound that killed him. That's what Jess said anyhow, she said that it wasn't possible, but I think she was just ruined by it, wouldn't let him go. Strangest thing though, the people who paid for the funeral demanded the coffin to be shut. Jess didn't have any say, poor girl, probably because they weren't married yet."

"Who paid for his funeral?"

"Now that you mention it, I don't know." "Well, do you think he's dead?"

"I don't want to, but I do, I mean it's been a long while and he ain't come back yet. Trust me you couldn't keep him out of this diner if you tried. He loved everything here, the pie, the diner, even my coffee, but if he is alive, the one thing that would've brought him back is those three."

"Well then, maybe she just has a thing for Johnnys."

"What do you mean sir?" "My name's Johnny."
"Johnny what?"

"Johnny Valentyne."

The chef's expression dissipates, as does his smile. Something I said really angered him, and now he looks like he wants to beat the shit out of me. Black and blue.

"That's not funny, you'd better not have told her that. Son, you've got a problem, you know that? I have a damn urge to kick your ass, guns or no guns."

"Man, do I look like I'm kidding? I'm telling you the truth, I don't see the problem with my name being my name. Anyhow, you'd better get in line for a shot at me."

"Now that's got to be, I mean you can't be...that has to be just the strangest damn thing. Her Johnny's last name was Valentyne. But not like the holiday, it's spelled V-a-l-e-n-t-y-n-e,"

"That's the same way as mine. Hell, maybe I'm that Johnny, wait, she would've probably been more excited to see me then, eh?"

"Well, I can tell you sir, you don't look like him.

You act like him, but your face is all wrong."

"Oh thanks, well I mean it could be worse, eh? I could be dead, like her Johnny."

His expression turns almost sour and then subtly with a smile a single tear rolls down his fat dimpled cheek while his color lights with rose.

"I was wrong. You are Johnny, her Johnny! I don't know how and I don't even believe it, but goddamn, your face is different, older maybe, but you're him, you've got to be. I've never heard anyone say that line other than Johnny, and I've heard it a thousand times, and it came from one person, and only one person, Johnny Valentyne. Jesus, Johnny, it is you? What did you do to your face?"

"Man, what the hell are you talking about? There is nothing wrong with my face. You know me?"

"Do I know you? Of course I know you. Down at that table is where you and Jess used to eat when you came in. Plus, I've heard that line answer every issue that ever got thrown at you, only used when shit got serious, ha, I mean it could be worse eh Johnny, you could be dead – but you're not."

When he ends that sentence, I remember him.

The chef's name is Charlie.

How did I forget him, this diner, this town, and all of them, the people who loved me? I smile, I just sit there and smile, while he tells me stories of me, stories when I lived here, when I was happy, when I was part of this place, and slowly but surely, I remember, not everything, but with every story a memory returns, and he's right, I'm that Johnny. I'm speechless as he goes down the grocery list of stories, stories he remembers, stories he expects me to remember but all I do is give a wide smile, and I nod, I nod until my neck burns.

"Have you seen anyone besides Jess since you've been back?"

"Nope, just her. And even then, I didn't even know who she was when I saw her, it's sad really. I don't even know what I'm going to say when I see her again – if I see her again."

"Then you've got something to keep you going, keep you fighting, don't you?"

"I suppose."

"You suppose, what do you mean you suppose? Johnny, listen to me closely boy. Whatever happened doesn't matter now, what matters is that you're back, you're alive, and she hasn't forgotten you, no one has. You did good here boy, a whole lot of good, and you'll make a whole lot of people happy when they know you're alive and well enough."

"Yeah, you're right. I mean...well you know the rest."

"Exactly. So, how'd you do it Johnny?" "Do what?"

"How'd you skip out on the slam, after you took care of those pill pushing morons, and their shit shack?"

"What now?"

"You're telling me you don't remember what happened, not even back then? I thought it was starting to come back?"

"My head is a mess right now, grey or all black or nothing at all, you know? Some memories are there, but some aren't, you talk about things I did, times I've had, and who I know, and most of it is a blur."

"It'll come to you, everything takes time, but you'll get there."

Charlie sits up, resting his stomach on the table, he looks at me with a warm smile, and nods. The nod implies certainty that I will remember him, this place, Jess, and my friends. He's sure, a lot surer than I am, but if he is, I may as well be. As I look at him, he continues nodding, bobbing his heavy skull, up and down, hypnotically.

My head pounds, it scrambles to compensate for all the new—well, old—images, places, people, and things that become memories.

I close my eyes, I try to concentrate, I try to find these memories, but something holds them back, the same three letters, and the same thing the letters stand for. Just remember violence, and I do.

I remember who I've killed, how I killed the and most importantly why.

To be honest I'm sick right now, sick of knowing, and sick of remembering, sick of me. I've destroyed families, crippled husbands, and made wives widows. I did all of this because I was told to, and I never spoke up, I never said no. Mechanically, I've slain without regret or regard.

But the guy I remember, this Johnny Valentyne, he's not like this, he would've stopped himself, he wouldn't have killed because he was told to, he would've killed because he had to, because he was forced to, and I'm sick because the person I am isn't the person I want to be. I want to be Johnny Valentyne because he's better than me. I've just been walking in his shoes, borrowing his body, and leaving his life behind.

Things seem to take their place, I can recall certain times before the company, before I became their dog, and I remember things about my servitude, but something holds back the rest, the more I try to remember the more it hurts.

"Johnny, are you ok? You look ill."

"No, Charlie, I'm...I'm well, just not alright."
"Anything I can do?"

"Tell me more, tell me anything you remember of me, tell me what I did, and tell me where I can find them, Jess and the others?"

"Well, back when you, Manny and Max were working for Samuel,"

I cut him off.

"Doing what? Manny, that's one of my friends, one of the guys who didn't believe I was dead?"

"Yeah, you, Manny, and Max worked at the graveyard, Samuel's graveyard, well, digging graves. You were in rough shape back then, really rough shape, but you kept on."

Again, I cut him off, with a cigarette and a smile.

"Why was I in rough shape?"

"Bad relationship I guess, you'd been with the wrong woman for a while then, Laurie I think her name was, horrible habits, horrible attitude, but you stuck by her."

"Laurie, who the hell is Laurie?" "I don't know son, anyhow,"

He smiles,

"You guys came in one night looking like ghosts, talking up a storm, a heavy argument about something, those guys were trying to convince you to just walk away from whatever you were about to get yourself into, but you being you, left in a hurry, and that's the last time I saw you. A couple of days later, I pick up the paper, and there you are."

"Where can I find Manny and Max?"

"Ah boy, you really have lost it huh? Manny took over his parents' farm, off highway six, just down the road from here. You really don't remember?"

"No."

I throw two smokes in my mouth, light them up, take in one long breath and then I pass him one.

"Thanks."

I nod, staring blankly out the blinds. "Johnny, what're you going to do?"

"I'm going to make them regret what they did and what they intend to do. I'm going to dismantle them piece by piece until they stop sending people, and when that happens, I'm going after them, one by one, until no one is left."

Smoke is pushed out my nostrils in the visage of a raging bull before a charge. I smile.

Charlie looks up at me, squints behind those half-inch thick lenses, and smiles.

"'Cept you though, right Johnny?" I chuckle and retort.

"Except me Charlie, till I'm the last one."

"And then what? What do you suppose killing all those people will bring, other than more people trying to kill you, or the people you love? Johnny it ain't going to end that way."

I look at him, expressionless. Whether he's right or wrong, I still have to end this, and it is the only way I know how.

"It will have to Charlie, because they won't stop, they never stop."

"Then you're never going to stop, Johnny. Whatever they did to you can be undone with time, I promise, but it's going to take time, not more blood."

More and more memories, things flash back and forth. One of the most dominant reminders is how wise Charlie could be, even though he's a middle-aged, half blind, overweight, small town diner chef, with no aspirations to be anything other than exactly what he is. He's more intelligent than he should be, but he doesn't understand my situation, how could he?

If you need a cup of coffee that would not only change how you feel in that moment when you first take that near scalding sip, gulp, or however the hell you drink coffee, but that would make you look forward to that cup of coffee the next day and all days after, probably right up to the day that you die, then Charlie is your man. The same goes for pie, or anything you can fry, cook, or grill. But knowing the answer to my problem, if there even is a definite answer, well, I've got to look elsewhere.

Sorry Charlie.

This is where the fear starts back up because strangely, not a single cop has shown up yet. I'd think in a small town like this, they would jump at the chance to bust someone or fire a couple rounds.

It was a shit storm in here for moments and those moments brought little consequence, which brings me to a question, and that question is – where are all the locals? Where are the boys in blue, the block-walkers, the highway patrol? Anybody with a gun and a badge should've come long ago. But they haven't.

I then realize I should've knocked on wood. Maybe I should've kept those thoughts for later on, maybe I should've enjoyed the peace I had been granted, or maybe I should've shut up all together.

FIVE

As smoke billows from my nostrils, a gunshot has me paralyzed. Warm blood splatters on my face and Charlie's cigarette falls as his hands limply smack against the bench seat. A smoking hole in his forehead oozes blood. Conveniently, my guns are placed symmetrically to each other in front of me. All I have to do is grab them. I choke as I look into Charlie's dead eyes staring up at me, as if he's wondering why, why I haven't reacted. Charlie's corpse anticipates my actions and is disappointed when they don't come as quick as they should.

"No."

I whimper as I stare into his eyes, tears in mine, hanging on the lids and waiting to fall. His eyes fade color and gloss over, the river that flows from a new wound begins to slow, and the shooter's reflection is clear in the dead pools of his pupils. He's dead before his head hits the table.

My stomach twists, my nerves wracked, and my head is filled with choices. Few but accurate choices, choices that will decide right here whether I live or die. As the two men slowly enter the diner with their guns raised directly pointing at my back, I'm still. Now, I'm forced to abandon fear, rationality, and a general reason to not piss these guys off.

The only friend I had, my only witness, my only chance at explaining this, is dead.

Charlie didn't deserve this, not any of this, not one damn moment of this entire chaos should've been his business. But it was, and his sincerity and assistance kept me alive. He kept me from dying and I should've employed that same service. He didn't have to die. Because of my actions, he did, and that's life.

He trusted that I wasn't one of those guys murder anyone and be able to sleep a full eight hours kind of guys. But I was. Yes, I may be different in many aspects from these cold-blooded bastards but at the end of the day, I'm just like them. Except recently, I've had a change of heart.

So, in this moment I had become not one of these two, I had become a guy who wouldn't shoot a man, an unarmed man before he even got the chance to lay eyes on me. I've never been a coward, and I don't intend to start.

My face freshly painted red from his blood justifies me in returning fire before I quickly become like Charlie. Staring blankly back at Charlie because I allowed myself to be shot in the back again for the second time today. No. Not again. I smile at Charlie as a tear rolls down my face, and a word doesn't make sound.

"Sorry."

Charlie's head falls with a moist thud, sending blood across the table painting the clean white surface crimson. His coffee falls as his body goes limp. The black river floods the surface area with a steamy layer.

Within seconds, the coffee and blood have diluted, flowing towards my guns.

I'm motionless and I desperately fight off the temptation to grab my guns and retaliate.

I fight the urge to grab them and just spin to face them, unloading both clips into two faceless men. But logic, cold, accurate, and safe to say I'm dead with that action logic says survival is less possible than probable.

If I move, I'm dead. That's just how simple it becomes.

These guys, despite my hatred, are skilled enough to rip me apart as soon as my hands go for my guns, the guns that sit in front of my coffee, helpless. I'm nervous as I hear them approach cautiously with their guns locked to the back of my skull. I embrace the sound of each foot step towards me, I just prepare, and internally my body cries out to move but I stay absolutely still.

That is until something suddenly falls, bouncing from my feet to the floor, and before it stops moving.

They unleash war upon the booth I'm sitting in. Instinctively I fall, I just let go and fall, without thought or attempt to catch myself.

I fall straight down under the table and hope. The sound of their Ingrams deafening as they begin to spit bullet after bullet into the booth I'm huddled under.

I curl into a ball as the booth begins to come apart like a target at a heavy artillery firing range. I hear the sound of casings bounce on the floor in the rain of bullets. I'm down but am I out? Suddenly a thought, badly timed, and possibly not important – what fell?

As I curl, center to the storm, as debris, coffee, napkin bits, and pieces of wood rain on me, I see it. Charlie's Remington sawed-off shotgun. Still loaded, it comes as a sign. This is justice. I grab it quickly and pull it close. As bullets tear around me, somehow every last one has missed, unless I'm hit, and I just don't feel it yet.

They walk closer spraying down the surrounding area, with every bullet, a casing burns across the floor, now a sea of shells. They're getting far too close but then again it could work to my advantage. Then something shatters through the silent thunder and the sound is just echoed by another click.

The sound of empty cartridges comes as a blessing.

I place my feet on the table support beam, preparing, tense, and then readied, I kick off strong. I slide across the floor with a trail of casings under my body, dirty, hot, bullet casings mixed with a cocktail of debris. Just before I hit the surrounding bar kitchen, I take aim and fire. A dragon breath stream tears from the barrel and the butt of the shotgun cracks my ribs. The pain wakes me just in time to focus on the spread that tears through the legs of both men.

Screaming, they fold to the floor, bones torn, and blood rushing. But I'm winded, lost the air I needed to move, and I desperately need to move. Both parties need to recover, my case not as bad as the squirming surprised men. I look doubtfully upon their attempt to stand back up with a thousand searing pellets lodged in their lower body.

Time, it's all I have now. Unsure of how much time before one of these guys has the strength to reload his gun, and begin to burst fire in my direction, re-littering the floor with hundreds of bullet casings, bullet casings that are now lonely without their slugs.

Holding my newly cracked ribs in one hand, and the smoking shotgun in the other, I rise.

Click, a fresh magazine finds a home in a warm Ingram Mac ten. One of my adversaries shrugs off the pain of a couple hundred burning pellets riddled into his pelvis. Grunting, he stands, raising his gun at me and a smile begins to twist on his face. His eyes burn, locked on me, he cocks the Ingram and readies to pull the trigger.

I don't even freeze, think, or pause in my action. I kick off from the ground and fly towards him with the empty shotgun swinging. A sick crunch followed by twitched out rounds firing off in the air. The butt of the shotgun catches his jaw and with a sick muffled grunt his eyes roll back. He loses balance and then falls like a cement bag being dropped.

This guy is out cold.

His Ingram spins at my feet as his partner looks up at me, dazed, with a subtle hatred in his eyes. He has one thought repeating in his mind, and that thought is, kill me. He reaches for a magazine stuck in the holster at his belt, trying to stand to one knee. We're both frantically trying to arm ourselves, but I'm already on my feet.

When my knee hits him, he's unprepared, he loses grip on the magazine, the gun, and his ability to stand.

As he hits the floor, I'm standing over him with the shotgun over his head, my knee has him heavily disoriented. He spits blood, dizzy, he tries to shake the blow but before he can react, the butt of the shotgun crashes down on the back of his skull.

As his face bounces off the floor, his nose sickly cracks, more blood as his bridge splits open, followed by more blood as the butt is quickly returned to the same place. I just return the butt again and again to the same place. As I force the gun down, I put my entire body down with the blow just like a hammer. Eventually he stops struggling, his body ceases to shudder, and then finally he is dead.

Still and motionless but I continue the assault for seconds before finally agreeing to discontinue the attack to his skull and slide to the floor beside him.

I breathe in so deeply my lungs burn. My shirt is ruined and almost completely dyed red from blood.

What a fucking way to start a vacation. Then suddenly I think, actually allowing some thoughts to fire, I realize, this isn't a fucking vacation. I was here to kill someone, and I realize now, I couldn't, because I know now, I don't want to kill the person I was sent here to kill.   I'm in the shit now, knee deep and with no way out apparently, but soon, or hopefully soon something will present itself.

I'm capable of reason now, and I'm able to discern the one single reason as to why this all ensued.

It's because I couldn't shoot her.

Everyone that walked into this restaurant after I had been shot in the restroom is affiliated with my late employer. I understand now why they've gone to all this trouble, and I guess I'm worth it for what I know, and for what I did. I don't think trouble can go a day without me; in fact, I think trouble is in love with me. I'm now afraid, impressed, and sick all at once.

My head spins, my body aches, my stomach twists, and my vision blurs. Despite how sick I feel I've said it, and I'll say it again it could be worse, I could be dead. But—and this is key—I am not.

Consequently, I've never felt so alive.

I rise slowly, breathe, and walk towards what's left of my table. Reaching into the rubble, I rescue my guns.

My eyes find light, gently flaunted by shaking blinds. I just sit staring out the blinds listening to the slow oscillation of my heart pulsating methodically, as my vision locks on ruby light from the sun. I holster my guns, sliding them into place, locking them tight. Digging into my pockets, I remove my Zippo, and pack of cigarettes. The cigarette pack is crushed, but the cigarettes are thankfully unharmed. With a heavy sigh I place one between my lips. I believe my wounds have finally clotted.

Disregard the fact that my clothes are irrecoverable, contaminated, and I'm left in complete disarray. Distrust, still question the events that ensued within these walls, and still unsure that this ends the story for the diner.

Retrace to right before I went into that washroom, look back and actually count the people. The people that were in the diner before it turned into this, this abandoned diner, empty of what it requires.

Right before someone cowardly shot
me with the intent to murder, murder a guy just trying to take a piss, have a bite to eat, and leave this diner.

But I don't want to leave; inside of me, a feeling, strange, but a feeling of warmth. I feel home here somehow, I've been trying to hate this place and everyone in it, but I can't.

I realize why I couldn't and why I was in the department store. I was there to kill someone, and then it dawns on me, what was causing me to remember, and why couldn't I remember before. Switching the place of my heart and stomach I'm sick, I was going to kill her, and I can't understand why, why her, why did they want her dead.

I could barely make sense of who I was until today, or maybe I never tried until today. I'm poisoned by thoughts and memories. They flood my consciousness, and make it extremely difficult to concentrate, but I let them. I need to know who I am. I spark the patient cigarette in my lips, take in a slow deep breath, and pace back and forth in the decrepit aisle of the inner diner.

SIX

That's when he moves, as I make the second rotation of the diner. The stupid bastard, who almost lost his head to an empty shotgun, starts to fucking move as he begins to regain consciousness. The first one to fall in the fight has somehow remained alive, despite my best efforts. I thought that the shotgun butt to the head would've killed him, especially with how much force I had put behind that hit, but he's alive and regaining consciousness.

I sigh, disappointed in myself.

The muffled, choking, clicking sound he makes when he tries to speak tells me his jaw is broken. His jaw shakes as he groans painfully trying to relocate it. I'm obligated to kill him, because he's contracted to kill me. It's not mercy because a couple pins in his jaw will have him right as rain. I wish there was another way but there's not. I know if I don't silence him now, he'll come after me again, and that's a chance I'm not willing to take.

These men only communicate in one fashion: green. They're cold, robotic douche bags that would kill anyone for the right price, I mean anyone, and that includes their own parents. Remorse must've been surgically removed at an early age. Concepts like sympathy and empathy are foreign to these suit and tie wearing automatons. They know they're only good for one thing because they gave up their life to do it. They've adapted to changing their identities like a shirt. I doubt one of these bastards even remembers their birth name. I mean I should know, I've been there.

Yes, this was my job, emphasis on was. Unemployed now and hell, I've never even had the heart to be one of these guys. I failed the job I was sent here to do. I just couldn't kill her. I suppose it all makes sense now or as close to sense as you can get. Too bad I can't get back my innocence...or maybe they are like me, medicated killing machines.

Clear as crystal, the result unchanged by my actions, and before I even reacted, the result would've been the same. The result is always the same in this line of work. Once a decision is made, it's unchangeable. If you fuck up, you're dead, simple as that. I can't exactly say simple because if that were true, I would be dead right now. I've learned that death is never simple and for that I hate him all the more, that's if death is even a man. Man or woman, I hate death all the same, but I seem to attract it.

As my adversary regains consciousness, my options are limited. I sit up on the bar kitchen with my gun fixed on his head. Painfully, he looks up at me, completely unsatisfied with the turnout. He bleeds from his mouth, nose, and he is stewing in a pool of blood which leaks from the shotgun wound to the crotch. A choked grunt as he realizes what's going on, surprisingly—and this actually has me stunned—his robotic son of a bitch actually pulls himself towards the empty Uzi which is only a few feet from his hand, painting a trail of crimson in his wake.

I again shake the sickness that grips my heart, ripping me from the prone position to one that's fixed and following him, gun locked on his head,

"Stop."

I bark from behind, a dying cigarette bouncing on my lip. My left arm is tucked against my bruised, throbbing ribs while my right arm is still patiently following his crawl. I'm sitting up straight with my legs crossed beneath me on the bar kitchen and I'm not moving for this guy.

Despite my request he still crawls towards his weapon and for a moment my patience escapes me.

"Hey!"

"You're fucking dead, Valentyne."

He grunts, letting his arms fall limp. His pointless journey ends just feet from his weapon and his hand is so close, close enough to continue, but he gives up.

"You don't look well friend. You know what? You could try just lying still and answering my questions before I pop you, because mercy seems to escape me right now. You can have it your way, you can continue crawling and lose more blood and take a bullet in the head or you can stop and tell me what I want to know."

I reply with the rose of amusement, stirred and unimpressed by his weak statement. I remove my arm from my mauled ribs and casually toss my cigarette into a pool of his blood. Hissing, its end extinguishes centimeters from his face. I look at him, trying to understand what reflects in his eyes, and suddenly I understand what it is. Fear, his eyes mirror fear because he knows I won't hesitate to shoot him if I go unanswered, and now he begins to contemplate my offer.

He considers for a moment maybe life is worth staying around for to see what's next. Maybe mortality didn't jump ship here. He's reading into this like I began to after being shot.

But his silence doesn't help me any, so my angry finger squeezes the trigger, and a bullet shatters the tiles next to his head as my patience exhausts.

"Why?"

A question I ask, even though I know the answer is not the one I'm looking for.

With a cool gaze and slow exhale, I await the response of my dying adversary. My voice rasp and thick, concern lost awaiting his answer, I ask again.

"Why?"

"What do you mean why? You know damn well why, Valentyne."

His response brings my gun level to his head. My eyes squint as I take aim, and a smirk finds my face.

"Whoa, wait."

He lifts his hand in front of my gun.

As if his hand will stop a bullet. Maybe he doesn't want to stare down the barrel, trying to avoid eye contact with the .45 caliber bullet, like staring death in the eyes and trying not to blink.

"All you had to do was erase that girl, and you could've come home. Insurance, Valentyne, it's always been about the insurance."

I'm unable to grasp the concept that I brought this on myself, and then I realize it's because I hadn't brought this on, they did. Long ago, and I'm just remembering what I came to finish.

"Valentyne, you know if you kill me, they'll just keep coming."

Staring up at me, he pauses before entering another sentence. His eyes are focused on my gun, again staring down the barrel. Knowing where the next bullet will lodge itself. Fear mirrors from his eyes, his expression empty because he knows he's dead, he just doesn't know when. At this present time our situations aren't so different. Despite the fact that I'm above this man, physically and metaphorically, I'm looking down at him. In this one and only instance, we see eye to eye.

At that moment we both realize there is only one resolution and that is one with a bullet. If he doesn't say something, he's already six feet under, and if he does, he will be. I pull the hammer back, frustrated. I've just relaxed the overwhelming need to know. His throat drops rough going down. He swallows the decision to speak, and words begin to form.

"Listen Valentyne, and I mean really listen to me. You fucked up. You put yourself in the worst possible place. You should've just stayed on the medication. This wouldn't have happened if you would've just stayed on those damn pills. Is she worth it? Is she worth dying for again, because man, look how long it took to make you. You actually believe you can break it?"

With that sentence, I come to a heavy realization. It wasn't amnesia, it was medication- induced memory suppression, and the medication

I stopped taking. The medication I was forced to take by my company so I could get the job done, the medication they force-fed me when I was nearly a vegetable, and the medication that was supposedly assisted my recovery. It is still hazy, but it's flooding back, and I can't comprehend it all but it's there, the truth is inside me pouring out and I'm struggling to make sense of it.

"Valentyne, you'll never be you again, you'll just be him. It's too late for that, too late to go back. You're dead, and I don't mean physically bud, I mean mentally, and furthermore, dead to the world. Jonathan Valentyne died seven fucking years ago. You aren't him man, you've killed the only chance at living you had. Man, and what, you think you can just go back to living that life?

There isn't life after the company, it's either you're with us, or you're dead. How do you apply what you are to everyday life, you're a fucking menace, a machine, a dog, and you'll never be anything else."

Suddenly, guilt and anger squeezes the trigger in reaction to the thought of my recently departed friend. Hot metal tears through his forearm, snapping the bone, a torrent of blood washes the floor. He grunts rolling on to his back sucking in air and then he screams. As my gun blows fresh smoke from its mouth, he stops screaming and looks at me with fury burning in his wide eyes.

"Was that absolutely fucking necessary?"

Spittle flies from his mouth as he stares at me clutching his forearm.

"That was for Charlie." I spit.

"Who the fuck is..."

His voice cut out by a bullet tearing through the back of his skull shattering the tiles below.

My sight slowly lingers on my dead friend, Charlie. I jump from the counter and on the way to Charlie's corpse I tear a tablecloth and throw it over his still frame. Blood soaks through the white cloth as it settles on the table. Something begins to settle within my chest, and it begins to calm my mind.

A short pause as I inhale, a thick cloud of smoke trickles from between my lips as my eyes focus on the night that has usurped the day. I stop moving and start thinking again. What did he mean by "you'll just be him"?

I have no idea what that means but I want to... How did I get involved with this shit you may

be wondering, good question, how did I get involved...I really don't have an answer for that yet, but I will, I promise.

Inhale, close my eyes, and wait. Things come back if I'm patient, and sometimes, well sometimes they don't.

I think I may have been like this before Grim found me, molded me, and made me good at what I do.

I've been an animal since the day I was born, maybe I knew it, but maybe I chose not to...

Not to accept what I was, what I am, what I was always meant to be.

I'm instinct, that's made use of a common mentality. Humans are just that, instinct, hidden, or lost along the unbelievably distracting bright road of society. Staring up and wondering who we are.

We live, we die, we fuck, and some of us, well only a small few, still kill.

So, I was sent, sent to sever what kept me from being that what they created. I was what they created, or at least unleashed, harnessed, and controlled.

The real question is why I still don't remember everything clearly, as crystal, bright as day, couldn't get more obvious, clear kind of clear. It is right there, behind the eyes, I close them, and it exists, but why can't I get all of it...think Johnny.

It's because, when I close my eyes, I just remember the violence, not precise acts I've committed, rather in how to commit it. I remember how to kill, without hesitation, like it's the end of all if I don't see it through. I guess for a tool, if you don't serve your purpose, what use are you? That's when they walk in on you, simply emptying urine from your bladder, not doing anything wrong, and they shoot you in the back.

Or back of the head, right through the lungs maybe, or maybe they'd put one through your back, straight out your heart, and then they would pry the bullet out of the wall, punch you with it, or jam it down your throat as some sort of sick calling card.

Or maybe they would just die trying.

It's difficult to accept, accept that everything has changed and all the while I've been right here inside, forced back by little colorful pills. Pills, that's it. It was always the pills and with this memory comes dizziness.

ANOTHER MEMORY

I begin to fall, try to catch the table and luckily my body falls into a nearby booth. I close my eyes as the room spins. As I close my eyes, behind them darkness I find and flashes, images and sounds form.

The next time I open my eyes, I find myself strapped to a hospital bed, which is something I find myself doing often. Not being strapped to a hospital bed but rather opening my eyes and finding myself elsewhere. The room is bare except a single man sitting cloaked by the shadow of the night side lamp dimly lighting my room from its position on the bare night side table.

I remember this now, but sadly, in this memory I didn't remember anything. Not even my own fucking name. I look to the window for reflection, and I see a young man who's wrapped in bandages, not completely, but heavily enough. Some bandages are white, some are red, but the most frightening is his head his wrapped up the most, the medical board says headshot victim but his are eyes open, this man, should be dead but isn't, this man, is me.

"Shit kid, you put up one hell of a fight, even with a bullet in your skull. Do you know where you are?"

"No?"

"No? You're a funny one boy, quit playing around, okay?"

My instincts kick in. "Don't call me boy, okay."

He lunges from where he sitting, leaping on to the bed and grabs me by my already bruised throat.

"Listen here you little shit, I don't care if you don't know how to die right, but you're going to work off the damage you caused to the company, even if you don't want to, you will. Shit kid, I don't know how you did it, but from where I am standing, you're not in any place to be pissing anyone off, alright?"

"Get your fucking hands off me."

I choke, spitting blood in his face. My thick crimson ricochets off his nose and slides down his right cheek.

"Oh, you little fuck! I'm impressed. I don't even want to know what kind of bitch pushed you out."

He says wiping the blood from his cheek with his sleeve. This greasy-looking bastard keeps his hair in a topknot, a thick black mess, aged grey. He's got a five o'clock shadow that hasn't seen the sun in weeks. This guy is pale, so pale it actually gets under my skin. I can't break his stare, staring at me from those leather bags that circle his blue-grey eyes. He wears something that clashes from the eighties that tried to reach back to the seventies but lost its way in between. His collar pops from under a pale brown leather jacket, with a nest of chest hair escaping the front of the collar, like roots escaping solid soil.

I was ready to punch him, but I realize I'm strapped too tightly to the bed to get anything behind the hit and even if I wasn't, I doubt at this moment I would do any damage. My arms feel like someone jumped on me while I was unconscious, and this same feeling resonates through the rest of my body, but painkillers smother it.

His eyes don't leave mine as he inches in, grabbing the tube for my IV pouch and as he does this, he quickly removes something from his pocket while lurching forward and whispers something in my ear.

I'm extremely disoriented but I still try and move, and despite any actual value in my attempt, it's an attempt, nonetheless. He now holds a syringe that's filled with a clear liquid, and he slowly begins to inject it into my IV. His lips barely move but I catch his sentence right before the needle makes it completely into the IV socket.

"When you wake up, trouble will be your only friend, but if you're nice we can make sure you make it out without seeing the inside of a jail for the next twenty-five years, so you may want to work on your people skills."

After emptying the syringe, he grabs the patient information board and switches the sheet. He smiles, as my eyes fight to stay open, I can feel something, something begins to take hold of me, and I can't fight it. Synthetically embraced, I'm now uncontrollably dizzy. Whenever I move, the room and this strange man haze in and out of light. My eyes can't stay focused on one thing, or I grow ill. So, I allow myself to be taken by this strange drug. The man's voice seems to be in my head, I can hear him speak, every sentence smoothly transfers my thoughts, and my full attention stolen by his sharp tongue.

"Listen closely Johnny, because this may save you. You're a convicted murderer, they have evidence on you that can put you away for not just one, but two life sentences, but we can help you escape these charges just like last time. All you have to do is play along but any resistance will be met with severe consequence. You have the power to not only save your life, but hers, do you get me kid?

You should've taken the money and just forgot about it, but you had to fucking come after us, man, don't you ever learn?

Anyways, this is how simple it is. You have two very concise options, and it's one or the other or nothing at all. Your first option is to spend two life sentences behind bars with very bad people, and with your looks, you'll be the belle of the ball or you can willfully forget and we'll get someone to take your place on one simple condition, you submit. When you wake up you won't remember me, so make your decision, and make it quick because you're leaving reality faster than I can speak."

"Leave her alone or I'll..."

My last words before I lose consciousness, even though I know he's lying.

"I'll take that as a yes." My eyes shut and light blinds me from behind my lids. I can't focus but I can hear. Whispers and sounds all around me, I can feel pain, pain from my wound. The wound on my skull bleeds. I can feel a knife trickle down my scalp, removing the flesh. I can feel a sharp motorized edge slice through my skull and with it I feel my body violently convulse.

My eyes open and I can see the red leather of the diner, and then I close them. I see a light haloing above me, and silhouettes around me. I then can hear voices.

"We're losing him, do something doctor!"

A nurse standing to my right screams at a man standing above me, her voice shrill and precise, piercing through the pain.

"I can't do this."

The man shivering above me drenched in my blood screams.

"I suggest you do it,"

Someone I can't see calmly insists.

After the sentence passes the lips of one of these medically masked, blanketed figures, I feel the end of every single nerve in my body cease with a single snip. I feel it surge and slice every single feeling in my body and the pain is so intense I want to cry but I'm immobile. I'm frozen, paralyzed, and without comprehension. This is when my eyes focus, and I find a horror I can't understand.

I see blood. They're painted in blood, painted with my blood. All of them stand motionless around me looking down. I see eyes widened behind small aquamarine medical masks. I can feel something erroneous about this entire memory, but only in what happened, not the fact but the action taken. This is where they first began to erase me, how I do know this, well I may not but that's what it feels like.

Simply with that thought I realize they changed who I was, not just mentally, but they physically erased my identity and birthed a new one, but why, why go to all this trouble for me and then the memory I've been searching for comes. It comes with regret and I realized how it all began. Regret and not without it. Something I did got me here and like a tape recorder being rewound, I return.

WITHOUT REGRET

Maybe I should've stopped her, spoke to her, said something, but the hour passes, and still she's gone. I don't mean she went out to get a bite to eat, I don't mean she's passed out, and I don't mean she left to find a new job, home, or guy to fuck, I mean she's dead.

This girl, the girl I now remember, the girl I used to love, is going to die, and there is nothing I can do to stop it. It's painful to watch myself, unaware of the events coming, watching a memory. Watching me.

I guess, now that I remember, it's best I start from the beginning.

There I was, sitting up at my kitchen table, in a house that I long forgot I owned. My thoughts, my mood, are completely and totally, for a lack of a better word, miserable. I found it sad when the world takes everything beautiful, and makes it disappear. I was staring at a gorgeous smile plastered black and white. This girl, this beautiful unaware girl, in this picture, didn't know she'd wind up on the back of a milk carton when it was taken, so she smiled, and all I could wonder, was why is she so happy?

Maybe she's got a great life. Maybe something or someone made her smile, but it definitely wasn't "I'm going to make this my 'in case I go missing picture' so it has to be a good smile" kind of smile. Then again, maybe she just saw things differently. She just felt like smiling, not that fake kind of smile when someone asks you to, but the one where you remember some good part of your life, and you smile. Knowing in that moment – the one you remembered – well, maybe you were just smiling, because you were.

"Johnny, where is my weed?" "In the box, where it always is." "Where's the box?"

"You'd remember where the box was if you didn't smoke so much weed."

"What?"

"Nothing."

My eyes nimbly venture from the missing beauty to my girlfriend, who isn't smiling.

She hasn't smiled in so long I don't think I remember what it looks like.

Laurie smiles.

Laurie, the one Charlie, said something about, and I remember that something not being so good.

It's not that she was a bad person, and even if she was, who am I to judge?

What do I mean was? Laurie is dead.

That's right, oh, I remember now.

Let's focus. One thing at a time, this is the day, the day she died, and I have to remember it.

And then I do.

I fiddle with the milk, trying to jam it back in where it belongs, somewhere between old food and something—well, something—I think may be watching me.

I close the fridge door. Walk over to Laurie,
kiss her cheek and start to exit the kitchen.

"Hey Johnny?"

I turn smiling, "Yeah Laurie?"

"Can you give me a ride to Sticky's?" I sigh,
"Yeah, come on."

Out the door and into my car, I sit down in the driver's seat, trying to smile, taking a deep breath, I pray for the ignition, and I get exactly what I expect, no sign of life.

"This car is a piece of junk, baby. You should just get a new one."

"Hey, this car just needs love. She's fine, just needs a little reassurance."

She sighs as I reach for my tools.

"Just turn the key when I say so, alright?" "Yep, I remember, because we go through this,

for no reason, all of the time."

I slide under the right front tire of my car. With my tool, my tool being what is left of my aluminum bat, I begin to bang on the starter. "Turn it."

"What?"

"Turn it."

"I am."

Still no life, I pull myself out from under my car, shielding my eyes from falling flakes of rust. I shrug.

"She's dead, sorry baby. You want to take the bus? You can keep me company."

"No, I'm going to stay home, later, love you." She goes back in the house.

At work, on my day off, my boss called me in, because somebody called him in, because someone needs to be buried, right away.

I'm standing outside his office, watching a silent conversation between my boss Eddy and this stranger, the one who's burying someone. There hasn't been a funeral, and there isn't going to be one.

This grave has to be dug, today. We don't have any equipment because ours is broken, and the rental place is closed, so guess who gets to dig it.

Yep, if you guessed me, you'd be right, congratulations.

See, what's strange is there is no funeral, which is odd, because there always is. When there is, the grave gets dug ahead of time, usually by a crew.

I dug graves for a living, with a couple of others, but they aren't here, it's just no buddies, no backhoe, just me.

These two don't say a word. He passes Eddy a brown grainy envelope, and Eddy smiles.

Son of a bitch, a brown grainy envelope, like the kind I get when—

When I remember this, I remember the envelope that's been stuck in my pocket since the diner. The one being handed over has my picture in it, no doubt.

But in this memory, it's just a grainy dull envelope to me, so I awkwardly turn and light a smoke, with my back pressed against the glass.

The door opens, the faceless man now bears a visage, back then I just glanced up from the flames licking the end of my cigarette, but now, remembering, I know this bastard.

"What're you looking at?"

I shrug and he smiles and walks away. Climbing into the front seat of a flat black Monte Carlo which I spent several very intimate moments drooling over earlier, he rolls down the window, and says,

"See you later."

At the time, I didn't care, and then Eddy walks out.

"Eddy, what the fuck?" "Yeah, Johnny I'm sorry," "Who the fuck was that guy?"

"You know I can't disclose that. And don't talk to me like that, I'm your boss."

"Get fucked Eddy, let's just do this."

"I know you don't give a shit, but thanks kid, I appreciate it."

My hand becomes a fist as I walk away, and from my fist out comes my middle finger, erect in all its glory.

"So does my wallet Eddy, so does my wallet."

I grab my gear, my gear being a shovel, my boots, and gloves. Gloves I won't be wearing for much longer and when I get where this grave needs to be dug, I dig. But the grave, the six-foot hole in the earth, the unused resting place I dug that day, was different. I didn't understand it then, but I do now.

My face is plastered to the bus window, watching the sunset, collapsing behind ruby clouds, retreating quickly from the ascending dark. I swear, some things you forget, and if you're lucky enough, you get to remember them. This night is definitely, for the most part, something I don't want to remember, but I continue because I haven't woken up, which probably means I'm dead.

The bus stops off the corner of my street, I leap out and walk with my headphones buried deeply in each ear. Back then, I guess, I wanted to be left alone, to go on with whatever life I may have had, undisturbed.

Not far from my house stands Billy K, my girlfriend's business associate, or that's what she wants me to call him. I still refer to him as her drug dealer, and when I do, it pisses her off.

He says something, I read his lips, and then I ask.

"Do I want to do what?"

"Get wet bro, do you wanna get wet?"

I push my headphones back into my ears and walk away.

He says something else, but I can't hear him, and I don't care.

Don't get me wrong, whatever pays the bills, and if you can keep your nose clean, then good for you.

But here's the thing, I don't give a fuck about weed, weed doesn't kill people, and you might want to say that drugs don't kill people. You might be saying other people kill people, for drugs. Fuck that. Some drugs kill, by themselves.

See, I don't like Billy, because Billy doesn't just deal drugs, he endorses them. He is a pusher, not a supplier, and there is no business in that. Another reason why I despise him is that what he began his career on, he no longer deals. Also, sometimes he accepts other forms of payment, that kind you have to pay out the ass for, and I mean that, literally. Billy doesn't sell weed; thus, he doesn't do business in my house. Billy sells the more seasoned stuff, the long-term drugs. The ones you depend on more physically than mentally. I don't like those drugs, so I don't like Billy. Simple enough, right?

I ignore him, like I usually do, because I just wanted to go spend some time with my girl before I had to go through this all over again tomorrow.

But tomorrow isn't going to be the same, just like the day after that, and the fucking day after.

Nothing will be the same after today. Not me, not this neighborhood, and especially not the place I used to call home.

I get in the door, and I dart upstairs into the bedroom.

But when the door swings open, I know now and I knew then, something was horribly wrong.

"Laurie?"

I stood there with my stomach in my throat as I stare down at her. She's motionless and pale. Her chest doesn't rise and fall with the sign of slumber. Her color is gone and she's like a statue.

A cigarette hangs subtly in my lips. As fresh smoke billows from my nose, I stare blankly at her. My hands fold fist and my knuckles bleach white. I feel something burn and it burns deep, rising from my gut. Every last bit of my body, mind, and soul screams for a reaction. I give nothing as tears well in my eyes and my teeth grind. Quickly, my anger dries my mouth and I'm consumed by unfamiliar emotions. I sit down and go for the glass of water on the table next to the bed but before I drink any water, I catch her lifeless stare and the glass shatters as it falls from my hand.

I throw the shards of the glass hard against the wall. At first, I deny this reality; I fortify that belief by repeating,

"This isn't happening, this isn't happening, this isn't fucking happening."

Quickly, I'm drowned by more tears. I'm blind and sick. I stand up quickly as this sets in. This is very real. She doesn't breathe. As tears run down my face, I catch a glimpse of something she clutches in her hands, pulled close to her heart. Motionless, I stand beside the bed, my eyes fixed on the object in her hands, and I know exactly what it is.

The feeling that follows is completely alien. I feel as if to scream, choke, and vomit. When nothing happens, I begin to cry uncontrollably. My tears blur my vision, and I bite my lip so hard it bleeds. I crawl on the bed, whimpering like a starving dog. My head stops on her stomach and my hands go to hers. I weep as I can feel the texture of a picture.

The picture is of us, and that picture captures nothing from this moment, and nothing of this world. It holds something that cannot be altered by this event. That picture is of us locked tightly in each other's arms, smiling. She loved that picture and in her final moments she clutched to it. Even when she couldn't breathe, she held on to the photo.

Her final thoughts were of us.

With that thought, I feel something new wash over me and it resembles acceptance, but I promise this feeling is far off; I'm just unfamiliar with it. I ascend to her face, the face that died of ecstasy, though she doesn't bare a visage of euphoria. Bile encrusts the surrounding edge of her lips, her hair's twisted into the sheets, and her once beautiful azure eyes decline their soft color for a white sick glaze.

My hand trembles as I close her eyes, and my sobbing becomes wailing. I cry, repeating,

"Baby...baby...please, please wake up baby,"

My lungs burn fury and something begins to rise, but the sound coming is patient. I reach for the phone and call the ambulance as I sit on the corner of the bed being consumed by some strange force. My body tightens. My voice is void of emotion, hollow and monotone. My brown eyes redden as I look through the blinds. All I can see is shit, bright and disgusting shit on the streets below. The patient sound then rises as my eyes catch sight of Billy.

A sound tears from my lungs and punches through my closed teeth, scorching my throat. It pulls me from where I sit and guides me. I can't stop it, I know what I'm about to do, and I can do nothing but watch...concern for my actions escapes me.

The phone speaks: "Sir? Are you there? Sir...," I'm out the door.

My front door buckles from the force of my foot. It tears from the hinges and hangs as I hit the sidewalk. I corner my house and catch sight of Billy K standing on the curb calling out to some girls across the street.

Those shameful words are his very last. Billy turns, catching a jackhammer punch square in the teeth.

Before he falls, I catch him by his exaggerated diamond encrusted necklace that hangs mid-torso. I wrap it around my hand and quickly return another blow, pulling him into the hit. He's stunned, bleeding, and missing a large amount of teeth. But he still breathes, so I keep punching him, accurately returning the hit to the same place. My hand is already swollen and painted in his blood. Teeth fall like pebbles and after the seventh or eighth hit, his chain breaks and he falls hard to the concrete, cracking his skull. But that doesn't discontinue the assault. Before he has a chance to gasp from the bloody orifice he used to call a mouth, I'm kneeling on his chest.

I pound downwards with nothing but primitive intent. I return shot after shot after jaw breaking, teeth shattering shot. With every solid hit, I see Laurie's lifeless corpse lying in my bed and this drives me to continue without end. Billy's face disappears more with every strike, and he becomes unidentifiable. Cheekbones, eye sockets, nose, and mouth are all severely damaged. I stop suddenly but it's not from the realization that I'm killing him; it's what I must do to quench this hate. My hand goes to his throat while the other hand goes to his pocket.

I tear a bag full of bright colorful pills from it. I rip the bag of ecstasy open with my teeth and begin to pour the entire contents of the bag into Billy's shattered mouth.

"How does that taste Billy? You want to get wet eh Billy? How does that fucking taste?!"

I scream millimeters from his face, forcing the pills into his gaping bloodied hole. Billy's sad attempt to breathe causes him to swallow a mouthful of multi-colored pills. So, I begin to add more, more, and more until the bag is completely empty.

Billy begins to convulse, Billy begins to choke, Billy begins to foam, and then Billy stops breathing.

Billy is dead.

I stand and spit, trying desperately to calm my erratic breathing. I try to focus but focus does not come. I grasp for thought but only one thing comes. It's not control, it's not reason, and this does not stop here.

I try to restrain myself because despite everything that makes sense right now, I know none of my actions are sensible. They are undeniable. I can't stop and nothing I've done has assisted in ceasing this dead ended path. That's exactly where this will take me, to the grave, or the grave of somebody else twenty to twenty-five years down the road. But I don't stop. I disappear before the ambulance and authorities arrive.

I grab my shovel, and the gas can from my shed. I run through the fields of laundry, cloaking my venture, avoiding the public eye. I hop over ruined barbeques and stolen shopping carts. I traverse through wooden cubicle fences, and I arrive in a camouflaged backyard covered in overgrowth and trash. A broken door positioned behind a decrepit litter-filled dryer becomes my entrance into the house I shouldn't have come to knock on. But I did knock, and loud as thunder my fist did rap.

The door tears back and with a word, a pissed off rusty looking man stirred as an uninvited guest appeared. My shovel crushes down on the top of his skull. He folds flat to the ground motionless. I step over him and I'm in the living room. It's hotter than hell in here and there is only one reason for that. Somebody is cooking something, and it's not supper. I leave the can of gas by the door and proceed inwards. I'm calm as sweat beads down my face. I walk down the stairs slowly without a sound.

My breaths are few and far between, my chest tight, as my lungs scream for air, or even a momentary pause from this chaos. The air is stale and heavily lined with chemicals. As I turn down the stairs and reach the lower level of the house, I catch sight of machines. Strange large machines accompanied by a man wearing a white medical mask and latex gloves, well dressed and ready to cook. He's nervous but he holds himself well. He freezes when he sees me but before I can rush him, I get hit from the side. It's the pissed off guy from the back door and he's even more enraged with blood running down his face.

The force and surprise of the hit makes me drop the shovel, but his charge doesn't get very far. I bring my knee up hard to his chest, and with a crack he goes weak. The fury that still brews inside assists my violent counter. I wrap my arms around his neck and lift him upwards. Pulling his head up, I throw a violent hook into his Adam's apple, choking him and before he can react, my foot is planted on his chest. I kick off, bouncing from the stairwell back down with another crushing punch. He again falls. But this time I don't make the same mistake of leaving him there. I leap upwards and kick down with all my weight in the same place. The snap tells me this man won't move again. Limp and bloody he now remains.

When my eyes go back downstairs, the man in the white mask is holding a small handgun. He just stands there pointing it at me. He doesn't move, and the only movements he allows are shudders. I stare back at him, unbroken.

I crack my neck and hands taking a slow step down and then down another stair. My shoulders lurch and my eyes never leave him. I simply walk down the stairs and towards him without a thought. I don't hesitate, I don't stumble, and I don't sway.

Finally, when I get directly in front of him, he speaks. But before words form a sentence, my hand grabs the gun, and my elbow finds his nose. I bury my elbow in his face and push him backwards. Limply, he releases the gun and falls to the ground, unconscious. With that, I walk back up the stairs and immediately throw the gun in the sink. I make my way up the stairs to the second floor of the house now. I see my gas can as I ascend. Smiling, I await another attacker. No one else comes.

This house is empty. Wait, no, someone is here. I hear breathing. Not shallow, scared, trying to hold your breath breathing. I mean this is someone just allowing air to leave their body and then sucking it back in. I follow the sound to the second floor and through a door ajar, I see a girl on the couch. Angelically, her hand hangs off the couch, slender and thin, marked with years of damage. Not from needles but from abuse. This girl, like Laurie, was just in the wrong place at the wrong time. This is the girl from the milk carton, the one with a beautiful smile.

She is unconscious but alive, barely breathing, but high. I lift her still frame from the couch effortlessly. I turn and walk back down to the first floor, out the front door, and into dusk. A dimly lit driveway calls out to me right across the street and just beside it, I see a flowerbed. Exhausted, the pain seems to come from the dark, eating its way up and out of me. Each thought becomes a tear. I soak up these dying dreams with a grunt and shake from the saddened hold. I fight the feelings that eat at my heart and draw the breath from my lungs. I find strength from something I didn't know existed. The light at the end of my dimly light hallway, guiding me, and I can't ignore it.

I can't leave the innocent to die, not again, and this would be the right thing to do in all the wrong I've accomplished today. She lives.

I lay her down on the small bed of flowers, immediately returning to the house to finish what I started, and to cease this place from doing further harm. It wasn't noble, it was just. I had to do this, to end this anger, to silence the voice that cries to avenge her.

Violence, murder, and fire may not silence my mind from remembering but it will—and I promise this—it will at least ease and distract. I find myself back in the house and even with the chill of night the heat remains.

My hair clings to my face and sticks around my eyes. Sweat blurs my vision as I begin to empty the can of gasoline on the carpet of the first floor. I walk down the hall, past the basement and I splash more and more. Soaking the walls and floor as my gas can runs near empty, I reach the front door. I let the remainder of the gas run out on to the welcome mat and the can is empty when I step over the threshold.

Standing on the porch, I release the longest sigh of my short-lived life and remove my cigarettes and lighter from my pocket. I throw my hair off my forehead and pull it back, receiving a blast of cool summer wind. I throw a smoke in my mouth and light its end. Staring into the flame of my Zippo, time stops.

Inhale.

For a moment, I find peace. Only for a moment and as quickly as that moment comes, I close my eyes and the peace is gone. Laurie is just behind my eyes waiting for me, reminding me, and she won't let go. I don't want to look at a world that destroys its beauty, masked by pleasure, suffocated by bile. I know not to blame myself, but I can't help it. I can't help thinking of her, I can't help her, and it kills me.

I'm a dragon blowing smoke from between cracked lips, flared nostrils, and with a flick of my arm, I create fire, tossing the flaming Zippo into the house.

Exhale.

The smoke escapes my mouth and nostrils, to be engulfed by the open portal. When my Zippo hits the floor there is a moment of silence. Deep, impenetrable silence. When I blink, fire welcomes my sight. Blind. Seconds after that, something loud, so deafening, is the last thing I hear. The force of that noise sends me flying backwards, closely followed by a hurricane of shrapnel. Fire, debris, sharp daggers of wood, and knives of glass find home in my burned body. The heat so intense, my eyes barren and burning; the fire is the last thing I see. The fire that reached out from the doorway to embrace me, and then to feel the pain from hundreds of foreign objects that cook inside tiny wounds. All that is left is darkness and pain as I smash into something solid, something concrete. I gasp for air but within moments I lose consciousness, and I'm lulled to sleep by far off sirens, embraced by pain.

I'm dead.

No, I'm between memory and reality. I see flashes of Laurie and me. I see her smile as I walk into the bedroom. Her bright cerulean eyes sparkle, their color has returned, and she's statuesque with arms wide, carrying a proud expression that melts me. But with a rush of pain, that scene is gone, and my body convulses violently as powerful current restarts my heart. I grunt as I bite down hard into something rubbery, something to stop me from biting off my tongue. I see bright light above me, and shadows. I feel cold moist metal on my skin. Everything is still and then sharp current is released on to my chest. Images pass quickly and then I'm blinded again. I lose consciousness and I hear shouting. The words aren't clear. As my body crashes back down, the machine sends a shrill noise that deafens me, again I feel as if to let go. To peace I will surely find.

I see Laurie again. I'm mesmerized by her chocolate brown hair and how it hangs low past her neck. She sits up on our bed, allowing it to fall back slowly to a vertical position. From under the silky brown blanket, she smiles at me with those gorgeous blue eyes. The way she smiles, the adorable dimples, and how the beautiful freckles that cover her surround them shoulders and cheeks. Her soft peach skin is lace to the touch as she pulls me close, a warm kiss and then I smell her. I can actually smell her, and this smell had become my greatest addiction. Her smell removes the pain. I hold her tight as we share oxygen, breathing as one and for a moment, for an undeniable moment; all of those horrible things didn't happen. Sadly, a more painful current steals her sweet image suddenly.

"Hold on, please hold on," a soft voice pleads from outside my unconsciousness.

My scorched lids rip open and I'm being rushed down a white hallway, surrounded by unfamiliar masked faces. My vision isn't clear, my mind is still clouded, and I'm suffocated by pain. Every single inch of my body confirms one feeling and that feeling is agony.

Just miserable and undeniable torment. I cannot fathom life like this, but they somehow pull me back from death. Time and time again. Even when I lose the images that are my reality, even when the pain is so intense I pray for death, I remain alive but shrouded in the dark. I see nothing for what feels like eternity, and for that eternity, I do nothing but remember. For days I hear voices questioning, trying to discover the events, and they request information. I give them nothing except bitter silence, accompanied by the occasional moan for pain killers. I'm strapped down to a bed, under constant care, and yet I feel nothing. I find no solace, I can feel tears, but I can't find the sadness that brings them.

I'm numb and blind.

When I'm healthy, I'm brought daily to interrogation rooms by different officers. Shipped from the hospital like a package and then returned. I remain without words, emotions, or signs of life.

They ask questions, questions about Billy K, and if I knew what happened to him.

I say nothing.

They ask me about the house, what happened at the house, and why was I found outside.

I say nothing.

This goes on until Laurie's funeral, which is the only place I went besides the hospital and the police station. Her funeral was the last day I wore my bandages.

I sat in a pew alone wrapped up tightly in white bandages, wearing a black suit with a white dress shirt and a shitty old black tie. When they bring Laurie out, I'm escorted by a priest to her casket. With my right hand I find her face. My throat closes and with a sick grunt, I tear the dressings from my eyes. As tears fall fresh from my lids I see her face. The first thing I've seen since the fire and she's literally, with all meaning of expression, a sight for sore eyes. As time expires too early, just like this still beautiful girl, the pallbearers come to take her. I watch her leave my sight for the very last time.

She's gone.

I'm escorted by police from the funeral to my final interrogation. One and only one officer interviews me. My lawyer sits beside me wearing the brightest smile I've ever seen, while the officer is flushed. She's frustrated, and holding something she can't accept. She starts a sentence but,

"Tell him,"

My striped suit-wearing lawyer says, lacking any signs of patience.

Somehow, and without her understanding how, I'm a free man. The only witness was the girl I left on the flowerbed who was unscathed and extremely grateful. Billy's death couldn't be linked to me because conveniently the fire that nearly stole my life burned off all traces of his genetic material and nobody saw me beat him to death. I miraculously left nothing behind. Everything that linked me to this had been incinerated. Despite my motive, despite clearly being the person responsible for all of this, and despite how dedicated the prosecution was, I was released, and all charges were dropped. As the female officer finished her sentence, she choked in disbelief.

Back then, I didn't care, but as I remember, I have to agree. It doesn't make sense that I was freed, which reminds me that everything comes with a price, especially freedom for the guilty.

My lawyer escorted me back to my house. He dropped me off at sundown. He gave me some cash and told me to get some rest. I barely listened to any of this, the court case, the news, how people praised me. I didn't give a fuck.

Being imprisoned wouldn't have been any different from the days that followed, knowing Laurie was gone and that the paramedics were far too late to pull her from the clutches of death's embrace. It didn't matter if I was a hero or not. I live somewhere between memory and reality. I was tortured and punished by my own mind. I begged for peace, but I could find none because living without Laurie was unimaginable then and it's impossible now. Then I realize she sleeps six feet under, and I buried her.

I'm disgusted with life, with allowance, and with the end. Not just the end of Laurie, or how it came. I'm sick because I had to learn how to stop loving so maybe I could live again. That was the sickest part of life, teaching myself not to think of her, training myself not to love.

I found little gratification in what should've been a triumph, a long-awaited victory. My vision returning was a miracle, having barely a scratch except for minor surface scarring was unexplainable, and walking out of the hospital a free man shouldn't have happened, but it did. That list should've brought me satisfaction without end but the greatest accomplishment for me would be to accept that Laurie is gone.

I sigh reluctantly as my hand goes to my doorknob. I freeze suddenly as someone from behind me calls my name. I expect bullets to tear from my back or a weapon to cave my skull in, painting my door red. But the voice is soft, welcome, and somehow familiar.

I turn, speechless, as the girl from the flowerbed stands there, smiling. She looks relieved to see me. She runs up and throws her arms around me, holding me tighter than I've ever been held. I smell her and suddenly I realize she had been there. She had been with me the whole time. She was in the ambulance while they restarted my heart. She had been there, watching over me at the hospital, holding my hand, talking to me, and trying to find life in my lifeless vessel. She stayed with me the whole time, without question.

I try and hide my face, I try to pull away, but she holds on. She forces me to look into her eyes, eyes that can only be described as color within color. Her eyes are gorgeous green eyes that fade into hazel, swirling the edge of her pupils. With those eyes, she sees me for what I am in this moment. Not for my crimes, and not for my mistakes. She holds me tightly for so long, anticipating reaction, awaiting something she's certain of, and then it happens. I collapse in her arms. I fall to my knees and cry into her stomach. The pain returns but it's different now, its relief, its comprehension, and it's something I couldn't understand until this very moment.

Finally, I understand that I suffered long before Laurie died, despite my reaction to her death, and that I can't take back what I did. Nor do I want to. In truth, Laurie abandoned me. Laurie had killed herself. The finality of her action was justification enough to end this suffering. I tried so hard to make her happy. I tried so hard to do what was right, and in the end, I tried so hard for someone who wouldn't try for me. It wasn't my fault. I didn't force those pills down her throat; neither did Billy or anyone for that matter. She willingly took them. Laurie may not have regretted anything but in doing so she nearly killed the one person who would willingly die for her.

Now in the arms of this angel, I cry. Not from the pain of losing Laurie, but from almost losing myself.

I mean, it could be worse, I could be dead. I will live one day, with or without regret and I did.

SEVEN

I did live without regret. I lived for a long time without regret, but now that regret has returned with my consciousness. I open my eyes, in front of me the stained red leather booth, faded and frayed. The diner exactly how I left it, disarrayed and destroyed. Every booth is mangled by bullet holes and buckshot.

Hundreds of casings litter the black and white sun-tanned tiled floor. The bar kitchen and the surrounding stools bordered by racing-stripe designed steel plates, shining light from the iridescent buzzing bulbs above. I sigh as I realize that I need to leave but I just want to remember everything. Stay still and think. So many feelings flood in one after the other, unending. Almost a decade of my life returns, and I'm shocked to know what I have done, where I've been, and who I am.

They took my face, changed it, and made it their own. I'm a branded killing machine that they helped shape. I've been used. I never had a say, but now I do.

Beside the washroom entrance is a dirty mirror with a clock just above it, ticking away the seconds. The sound somehow, I've drowned out until this very moment. Distracted, I continue. When I catch notice of the mirror, I approach cautiously, because all this time, unconsciously, I've avoided my own reflection. I knew, deep, deep, down, locked far away, was the true image of who I used to be. My old face, my real face, the face that isn't there. They somehow blocked my memory, not just one, but all of them. Surgically, they removed them. I didn't even think that was possible, but my mind is so damaged by meds, by memories, and by the lives I've stolen, it must be.

I was lying to myself this entire time and I don't even know if I knew I was doing it. There behind that layer of dirt is the face, my new face, the face she couldn't have recognized because she doesn't know it, and to be honest, neither do I.

I spit into my left hand and start to smear it across the filthy surface, pulling off a thick layer of brown mess with my palm. My eyes are the first thing I see, but when I see the eyes sockets, cheek bones, nose, jaw line, and chin, I freeze. My scars are gone, my birth marks, and even the dimples she loved, all gone. I try and see past this lie but the only things still mine on this face are my brown eyes. My deeply sad brown eyes that squint at this mug I've had plastered to my face. My next actions, not without sanity, but harshly unexpected, I throw my face into the mirror and let forth a sound as my face crushes the brittle surface, cracking it.

I can feel the cut slowly spread open under my left eye and fresh blood trickles down my face as I slowly step backwards, looking at the cracked reflection. My fingers glide across the wound, annoying it, more blood, and I stare at my hand letting the blood from the wound drizzle down my fingers to the floor. Each droplet explodes when it hits the tiles near my feet painting a small segment of the floor.

My eyes go back to the broken mirror, the hanging fragments swing from the air circulating in the room, and at any moment they prepare to break off and fall into several shards on the floor below.

But they don't, they just remain absolutely still. This is when I begin to systematically shut down, first my body, its lower extremities first, followed by the numbing of my torso, shortly tailed by my chest and arms. I drop to my knees hard—without the intention of cushioning the fall—smacking on to the hard diner floor with each cap. My knees should hurt, but they don't, as should the rest of me but I'm numb. I don't feel anything, not one thing, not in the slightest, not even in the smallest of sensations, like a slight change of wind direction.

I'm numb, and without a doubt, void of any, and I mean any, feeling. My arms slump and my hands relax. I blink at the sound of my gun smacking hard on the floor, sliding out of my reach. My mind slowly begins to let go, absolving any idea, thought, or memory that attempts to stir. My mind begins to cloud, or at least heads in the direction of the sky. I'm gone. Moments go by, and in these moments, these absent moments, absolutely nothing happens.

Then, like a whisper in an empty theatre hall, a sound slightly above me explodes. A chunk falls from the surface of the mirror, and as I look, time slows and nearly stops. As the mirror creeps in front of my eyes, planning to shatter just in front of my knees, I see a reflection, my face, and a figure just behind me in the background slightly to my left near the exit.

The moment in which I can't move is gone because my body lunges in the direction of my gun, as a bullet tears through the dirty tile floor where I was just moments ago. The mirror bit shatters on the floor just in front of where my knees were, and I'm on the left of the washroom doorway turned to face my shooter, with my gun raised and aimed.

A motionless index squeeze and a round tears through the barrel shattering the glass behind where the person is now no longer, and I toss my head frantically from left to right with my gun following, searching for an unbelievably fast opponent, but no one is there.

"What's happening to me?"

I say out loud, hoping for a response, praying that I'm not crazy.

This is where my mind goes, pause.

I go limp and stare at the night beyond the newly shattered window, moonlight seeping in, staining the diner tables with its clean light. I blink, and as I breathe, I hear a click. The sound of what resembles a clock, the ticking, the seemingly never-ending ticking finally ends. The clock hands keep moving, but the sound is gone, and that means the clock is not the criminal behind the mechanical ticking, and if the clock isn't behind the clicking what is?

Through the shattered portal the night seeps in, darkness begins to enter, and suddenly every single light in the diner begins to dim, and then all at once disappear. The light is gone, and I sit quietly slumped against a wall, almost motionless, and in the dark.

It's odd being in this position, and I don't mean curled up, I mean remembering who you are, in the span of one day, even though who I actually am didn't exist to me, and to know now, who I am, well, let us just say, it's very discomforting.

I collect myself, my things, and I believe it's finally time to leave, nothing left here for me. I nod at Charlie, looking to the floor in a moment of silence, I gaze back at him almost expecting him to move, and when he doesn't I go for the door.

My hand rests on the shattered frame, breathe in, and out into the night I go. My hand cradles my holster uneasily. Just like my entire day here, again, something is very wrong.

Count the cars.

Why? Why do they matter? Something about the number of cars, why the hell would the number of cars in a nearly empty parking lot bother me? Maybe Johnny, just maybe it's because there are more cars than there are bodies.

"Shit."

With that thought, my attention is caught by a footstep; a footstep followed by another, then another, quickly followed by another. The steps are no longer steps, someone is charging at me. It is already too late to pull my gun, by the time I turn; I'm staring down the point of a very wicked- looking blade. Somehow, I've caught the attacker's arm, the arm that holds this knife,

the knife that is now no more than half an inch from my
nose.

My attacker and I are both shocked and surprised by
the speed with which I defended myself, and that he
can't move the knife forward or break my ironclad grip
on his wrist. Like him, I'm shocked that I caught his hand
and not the knife. I'm equally, if not more surprised
than he is, and that's my mistake.

Not retaliating costs, me blood, because he shakes
the shock and kicks his left foot into my stomach,
winding me. I stumble backward, losing my balance, and
the grip I had around his wrist. He quickly makes two
hard swipes toward me. The first barely licks the back of
my hand. The second swipe shreds my shirt, my crimson
dyed, not even twenty-four-hour old shirt, the shirt
formally known as my brand new fucking white shirt,
and when I feel the cut take over my stomach and a new
wound begin to bleed, I get mad.

As I gain my balance he lunges at me again, but this
time I catch him and not his knife and use his lunging
force to toss him. Flying between a parked car and van,
he recovers and turns to face me. He shakes the dirt
from himself before coming at me again. I move out of
the way at every vicious swipe, some miss, and when he
starts nicking away at my flesh, I have to consider a

different tactic. I've been circling him, but the wild swipes aren't easy to catch without finding myself on the end of his blade.

In desperation, I spear him into the side of the cube van. When his hands go up from the cracking of his ribs, I force the crown of my skull into his chin. Wrapping his tie around my hand I pull him downward into my knee, and that's when I feel his blade dig into my thigh.

I yelp, throwing him off me, releasing him and his shitty tie. While my hand goes to the blade sticking from my leg, he throws a punch that I don't see coming. His fist catches me in the left side of my jaw, which causes me to stagger, dropping to a knee. He leaps on me, knocking me into the right side light of the car parked next to the cube van, his hands wrap constrictively around my throat. I can feel my spine bend as my back dents the hood. In desperation, I tear the knife out of my leg and out with the blade follows a thick jet of crimson. I cut up against his wrists that squeeze the air from my lungs. Warm blood spills on my chest as he releases my throat.

I throw my head up hard, catching him under his chin. He stumbles back, shaking off the blow; he recovers, and throws a couple of wild swings my way. I duck and weave, slashing back at him, but he catches my arm, the arm that now holds the knife, and he throws his leg behind mine, sweeping me to the ground. Now he's on top of me again.

With both hands he pulls at the knife, trying to get it free, but instead of trying to fight him off, with my left arm, I pull down hard, and bring him into it. With a sick plunge, the knife is lost in his chest, and I feel him bleed out on me.

With this wound his strength leaves, he releases my hand, and with eyes wide he stares at me, surprised. I roll him off me. He lands on his back, coughing up blood, sprawling out like a turtle on its shell. He stares up at the dark sky overhead, his coughing becomes gurgling, and then the gurgling becomes silence, and he's dead.

I stand up, shaking off the fight, and as I stare down at him, I can't help feel anything but sickness. I've been reborn and suddenly I have a conscience again. I know that this guy, like many before him, doesn't deserve remorse, but I still can't help feel it surface for taking yet another life.

Then again, this feeling could be exhaustion, knowing that no matter how many I kill, they'll send more.

That's probably it.

I turn my attention back to the dimly lit, mostly desolate parking lot.

I'm in the middle of nowhere, and when I say this diner is off the beaten path, I'm not kidding. The road that leads into the diner is about a five- minute drive from the highway. This beautiful diner, that once made the best coffee and pie, surrounded by lush forestry, will now decay in time, just like Charlie. Behind his diner there are fields, almost endless to the unblinking eye. Fields of blueberries, strawberries, blackberries; every fucking berry grows there, because Charlie put them there. Thick apple orchards surround these berry fields, and I remember this all now.

I also remember not far from this place, and not far from the highway, my buddy Manny's farm. One of my best friends, and I only remember him now.

Some friend I am.

It wasn't amnesia; it was those fucking pills, those little grey and black pills. They made me forget.

Suddenly, I realize I'm standing in front of my company car, the one with the dented hood. I've already got the keys in my hand, but I notice something, something very unlike me about this car, the door is unlocked. When it comes to anything that has the ability to lock, if I'm currently not using it, or my house, or even the balcony door in my old apartment four stories up, I would lock it.

Currently the driver's side door is unlocked. That isn't me, I locked it, I know it did.

Thank my anal-retentive obsession for details because something has been changed or tampered with, something that could possibly result in my untimely death. Mind you, it would seem to follow the way my day has been so far. It's time to find out exactly what's been done while I was trapped in that diner.

I drop to my knees and crawl around under the front end of the car, occasionally glancing behind me, trying to stay aware, waiting for another assault, but I continue searching. There are several signs that the car has been tampered with, but as I scan around using what little light I have, I can't find the source.

This car isn't worth the time or trouble, but I need a ride, and that's when I remember.

I recover the keys of the bathroom attacker from the depths of my pocket. Out comes the shiny set of keys; they twinkle in twilight, and the plastic car starter finds its way between my thumb and index finger.

Standing up, with a squeeze, barely pressing the small plastic button, something chirps from the other side of the abandoned cube van. I see headlights flash, signaling the ability to enter.

I slowly corner the cube van, and stop suddenly from the surprise, my eyes still unconvinced at the beauty in front of me. The stainless-steel grill of what appears to be a 1969 Zl-1 C.O.P.O 9560 Camaro, its flat black surface doesn't cast off a shine. Enshrouded by night, this metallic beauty stares back at me, waiting. Without its chrome grill, trim, and hubcaps, this car would be otherwise invisible at night.

To the driver's side I run, like a child, to Christmas presents. With my right hand I fling the door open; my washroom adversary had fantastic taste but made very bad choices. I sit down in the dark leather seat, comfortably welcomed by the sweet smell of clean car. I adjust the seat and let my legs stretch out, the pleasant sound of leather forming to my lower body is soothing, and when my head touches the head rest, I nearly fall unconscious.

This car, despite its power and fury of cubic inches per square foot, contains a restful, unbelievably tranquil comfort from the interior. My left foot finds the clutch as my eyes reopen, the key slides in smoothly without resistance, and the turn of the ignition almost feels natural. When this car's engine fires, I'm deafened momentarily. The sound of its purr, orgasmic. It roars with fervor, warding off lesser engines, rumbling with anticipation for the chance to once again assume its dominance over asphalt.

From my peripherals I notice something. Something I should've noticed when I walked out of the diner originally, but didn't because I was preoccupied by the guy with the long, serrated knife meant for my back, and after that guy, was beauty. That's the thing about beauty, once you lay eyes on something; it's hard to notice anything else.

There, no more than twenty odd feet from this car, hidden amongst shadow and shade, cloaked by the building I've finally fled from, is a car, but not just any car, his car.

The man from the hospital, the man from the graveyard, the man responsible for my recruitment into the company, the man who pretty much stole my life and identity, is sitting up in his car, across from me, smiling comfortably.

This man is Benjamin Sketch. Now, I only have two feelings when considering this man, he is evil and vicious. What little I know about him I don't like. I guess you rarely like your boss, but I fucking hate this guy, and

I'm guessing that right now, he feels the same towards me.

At the company, he's referred to as Mr. Sketch. That's how I know him, and nobody calls him Ben, or Benjamin. If you do, it's probably the last time you say anything to anyone.

Mr. Sketch, without any emotion, points at something, and without a moment's waste, I look. I'll be asking myself till the day I die why I looked, because he pointed to nothing. As my eyes scan around, I see lights flash from my peripherals, and I hear the sound of an engine nearly red line.

Impact.

The front end of his car momentarily molds with the driver's side of my car. Dazed for a moment, now if my hands weren't already holding the steering wheel, I'd be in the passenger seat. Luckily for me a twelve-point roll cage reinforces these doors, or I'd be dead. Mechanically, my right foot finds the gas while my left releases the clutch. The car jumps forward, and I'm gone as he comes in for a second ram, but this time he's greeted by the side of the parked cube van.

The car he's driving, which most likely belonged to someone else, has no front end, but this of course doesn't stop him. From the rear-view mirror, I see him reverse from the crushed side of the cube van and pull out after me.

Thankfully this car is fast, well let's be honest, it's a lot faster than his. He's far behind, but not far enough, and if it weren't for the moonlight, I wouldn't be able to see him coming. All I can see is a dark object gaining speed, no headlights, just impacted metal waiting for another chance to impact further into my car's bumper.

From the soft asphalt to an unpaved dark road I go, shifting furiously into next gear. My foot glides off the gas while my other sinks the clutch for a rough change as soon as I hear the car red line, it's time, and after the gearshift, I'm thrown forward, deafened by the sheer fury of this beautiful machine.

The headlights barely uncover this would-be road. Somehow, despite the absolute absence of memories involving this road, I navigate every turn, every bend, every hole, effortlessly, without flaw. I know every corner before they come. I've had to have driven this road a thousand times before today to have this kind of accuracy and I probably did, whether I remember or not.

Mr. Sketch doesn't share this knowledge, or cornering precision, because it appears—and let's not assume, but it looks like I've lost him.

Then again, the dust this beautiful machine continuously tears from the earth makes it impossible to be sure. I then realize the next turn coming is death to any other gear but second. If I don't slow down, I'm going off the road. With that, my left foot punches the clutch and my right foot cases the break as my right hand furiously downshifts. With my left hand I glide into the turn kicking up dust and debris, a smoke screen for the rear view. As I come to the sharpest point of this curve, my feet repeat the same mechanical process, while my shifting hand follows not far behind.

When this curves off into a straightaway, I'll be home free, or so I hope. I meticulously glance between the rear view and the road ahead, but the dust and the night hide the road behind. I'm without clarification. Overwhelmed with frustration, I throw the car into neutral, and my feet crush down on the clutch and brake. I intend to learn the fate of Mr. Sketch.

I need to know if he lost control on that turn, so I can find him unconscious, face pressed against the steering wheel, bleeding out. His only friends, glass, and broken bones, shortly joined by a bullet or my unforgiving hands snapping his neck.

He has to die.

I then realize, like a cat, this son of a bitch has nine lives. Why do I allow these mistakes, I shouldn't have stopped, because I now see emerging through the dust, the crippled front end of his car, and with the impact my face tastes steering wheel, luckily with the hit I let go of the brake. I quickly throw the gear from neutral to first, and jam on the gas, spitting blood out of the window.

With the roar of the engine, I find the second gear, and within seconds I find third. Like I said, with the straightaway, I'm free.

EIGHT

I speed down this empty dark stretch, racing towards the open freeway, but I know the entrance is sudden and the turn is sharp. One mistake and I'm going to be involved in a high- speed collision.

When I finally get to fourth gear, I know at this speed I won't make this turn, but I'm uncertain if Mr. Sketch will slow, or if he'll just ram me, so I continue flying toward the red line. With one hand free, I begin to buckle myself into the racing harness that substitutes as a seat belt. Under normal circumstances it would be a bit much, but considering my present situation, I'm quite comfortable.

When the road starts to curve, I know I should downshift, but I don't. The little gauge tells me I'm running out of rpm, reaching the maximum speed. As the turn starts to fork into the freeway, I can see light from my peripherals, but I don't slow down. I then notice from my rear-view mirror Mr. Sketch's car catching up. A strange whistling sound, almost like a high pressurized gas, that car isn't stolen, it's a company car, equipped with nitrous oxide, and this son of a bitch is catching up quick.

Suddenly light—blinding halogen light— reflects from my rear view, blinding me. Looks like his high beams still work. I knock the rear-view mirror down, so the light doesn't blind me, but the driver's side mirror casts the same light. I can barely see anything at all now, behind me, in front of me, or even beside me.

Remember when you were growing up? When you were a kid? How were you forced hour after hour to learn about road safety? Remember that line—the saying everyone's heard a thousand times—remember to always look both ways. Well, I guess on my endless list of mistakes, not paying attention to that fundamental rule is now one of them.

Sadly, before learning the true power of this classic mechanical wonder, before I get to know her name, I'm hit so hard from behind that I careen onto the open freeway at the mercy of chance, and let me tell you, chance is a bitch.

Before I can even redirect this poor beautiful machine, I see light from a different set of headlights, dug into the steel front bumper of a vehicle moving at about one hundred, maybe one hundred twenty kilometers, a vehicle which I can only assume belongs to an innocent night driver, and for that I'm sorry, because that vehicle isn't reinforced like mine, and I doubt I'll ever know the fate of the driver.

On impact, I see steel, body, and fender explode on the backside door on the driver's side of my car. I brace as best as I can as every window systematically smashes into raining glass shards. This once beautiful car is tossed through the air down an empty dark highway.

I can't recall what's worse, the disorientation of the car flying upside down to right side up over and over, or the car being torn apart slowly every time it returns with gravity's embrace to the unforgiving onyx below. It seems as if something continues to pull her along, dragging her, making sure she doesn't recover from this accident. I see the blinding lights of the cars behind, as the beams slowly grow dimmer and dimmer as we roll out of sight.

Finally, we stop rolling, landing on the roof, gliding down the black milky vastness of this empty stretch of highway. Sliding off the freeway and stopping hard against the wall of an underpass. This is how I lose her, this beautiful machine destroyed, irrecoverable.

Attention is important, especially in neglecting the finite detail of beauty; you'll lose it if you don't pay attention, because in this case, I'll never know just how amazing she is on a cool open highway in summer. This thought stirs another, and then another as I lose consciousness, hanging upside down.

I've been hand in hand with death so many times, so many times I'm only just beginning to remember, but what I do know, is I survive for something, maybe even someone. This car accident has dislodged the block and things return to me, even as I lose consciousness.

Death – every time I get close to it, I remember things, places, and people. I chose to go to the diner today, was compelled to it, to go there and remember. I focus on certain things to remember, certain things like my shirt, like the diner, and the creek. To remember things about where I'm from, who I am, and who I love, and I do.

I remember her now, completely.

Her name is Jessica Lorelei Mackenzie and she's the girl I love.

She's the girl from the department store, as beautiful as the first day I saw her. She was the girl from the flower bed, the girl that stayed with me at the hospital, she was the one person who loved me, and seemed to love me without end, and yesterday she sold me a shirt without knowing who I was. A white dress shirt, a white shirt that's now red with blood, my blood, and the blood of other people, that I'm still wearing, regardless.

That's why the shirt is so important.

As darkness takes me again for another trip back down memory lane, I grab at one question, why did they want me to go after her? Why does she have to die, and why the fuck would they have sent me to do it?

Grim Associations, that company I'm going to dismantle piece by piece. The contract-killing, money-devouring company that poses as a life insurance company whom I believe by now you've heard a bit about. They picked me up, sometime after I blew myself up, sometime after I settled down in my own toxic free life, unburdened by substance, and free of heart-breaking situations.

They came to me with money, money from Laurie's death, and the money belonged to me?

I don't remember ever hearing about her life insurance, but they insisted I take it, they told me I deserved it, that it would compensate my loss. Is that what money was supposed to do?

No, at that point, good old stubborn Johnny stuck his nose out, put it in places it didn't belong, and good old Johnny wasn't quite healthy enough for this. Keep in mind I just blew myself up months previous, and was recovering, sitting on disability until I was healthy enough to return to my job. I never got to do that, return to my normal life, because they tried to silence me, and it turns out, they couldn't.

Those men I killed at the creek, well, they weren't cops. They worked for Grim Associations. They did what I do now, or make that, what I used to do. At the creek, they tried to kill Jess and me.

They didn't quite accomplish that, but they came pretty close, because that wound, I received that day, the accidental gunshot to my skull, gave Grim Associations another option.

In the depths of my unconsciousness the truth reaches out to me. At first all I hear is humming, then my eyes open. The humming becomes ringing and then the ringing becomes shrieking. The shrieking becomes words, those words become my name, my name being screamed by Jess. She's screaming for me to wake up, repeating Johnny, baby, wake up Johnny, please baby, look at me, please baby, no baby, I love you baby, Johnny please, what have I done, Johnny.

I can feel her tears on my face, she cries and doesn't stop crying. She tries to pull me from where I lay, but I'm dead weight. I just lay there in the grass, blood rushes down my face from the gaping wound in the crown of my skull. My chest rises and falls but slowly my breaths become farther and farther apart, and then I stop breathing altogether.

She screams, a sound I never want to hear again, so loudly it brings me back to life.

My thoughts revolve around how unfair it is for her to see me like this, to see her cry, and all I want her to do is stop crying, and in one word she does.

"Run."

The tears well but don't fall, they just hang on her lids waiting for her. The ducts close because she's overwhelmed by confusion. She kisses my lips, shaking her head softly, protesting against my statement, pulling at my hair, kissing my face, and tugging for me to stand.

"Run."

Another conscious response has her crying, I'm alive, even though I shouldn't be, I'm speaking to her even though I should be breathless, coagulating. She tries to argue but in my stare, is my response, and with my last exhale she understands, and as my body goes limp, she lets go.

That was the last time I physically saw her, up until I purchased that shirt, and now all I want to do is see her again.

Johnny Raymond Valentyne died that day and the guy I am now took his place. With every hour that passes, I'm getting him back, getting back to me, and now I have to get to the company, before they get to her.

What does the company do? They choose people prone to dying, people who make bad choices, people who have drug problems, criminal records, and people who have a greater chance of dying and then these people are offered life insurance. But here's the kick, there's an incentive for accepting the contract. They pay you.

How many people do you know would turn down free money, money that will benefit you while you're alive? And then when you're dead, your family, loved ones, even your fucking pets are taken care of.

But here's the thing: the company profits, they profit quickly because people like me come like the reaper and take your life. Yes, your family gets paid, but you're dead.

Sound good?

No, it shouldn't, trust me. Just living, doesn't matter what you do, who you are, death comes later. Let it come naturally, because even if you think you're sure that you've got nothing to live for, well you're wrong, because something, someone, somewhere needs you.

Now, how they get away with all of it, how they fund this operation, well, I can only guess it started out small, and like all things good or bad, grew.

I know now the day I blew that lab and myself up, that lab had been used for the creation of my new life. It birthed those little pills that made me who I am today. The grey and black pills, the ones that helped me remember grey or black or nothing at all.

I became a construct of reality. That day in the hospital, the brain damage, all made my cognitive re-education possible, and with the entry of those pills, I became the company's killing machine.

Greyor Allblack, my name, for what I can only guess, the last seven years. With those pills, I forgot not just who I used to be, but I forgot the families I've destroyed, the people I've killed, the monster I'd become.

It was perfect, until they sent me here. Why, that is and will always be the question. Why would they send me here? If it was a test, I failed miserably, because from the depths of my subconscious Johnny Valentyne is still alive, somewhere locked away, but that door is now open.

I remember him now; me, who I am, who I love, and what I've done.

I remember the violence, but I remember everything else, and I know that is not what the company spent several years trying to erase. A mistake, then, not one of mine but somewhere in the company, I have a friend, or someone who sympathizes. Or maybe, just maybe, it was an honest mistake. Then again, in this business, you can't afford to make mistakes.

So, there is the only question, the one and only relevant question, why did they send me here.

That's when it kicks in, the little brown envelope, the one marked with Grim Association's initials, the envelope currently buried in the depths of my jacket pocket, attached to me hanging upside down in a car wreck. That is my only possible answer, but I can't reach it, because I'm unconscious.

That grave I dug, on the day I had forgotten about, the day I blew up that lab and myself – I think back now, and I think I dug my own grave. I didn't actually get buried, because I spent the next several years in a hospital with no memory prior to the surgery, but I underwent training, physical therapy, and cognitive assistance that really wasn't for remembering. It was more directed to forgetting, and remaking. But they taught me things, things that have kept me alive, combat training, martial arts, weapons training, ballistics and melee.

They worked with what I had, gave me new tools to kill, but why did they go to so much trouble? I think it's because I had a hard time dying. I mean, I blew myself up, and I'm still alive. I got shot in the head and I'm still here.

The day they found me bleeding out, alone and powerless, they brought me to their facility, the Southstone hospital. There, I got better, they force fed me pills, conditioning me to this life, but now, now I'm not that guy, but I remember everything.

What do I do now? I wake up, and finish what I started.

My eyes open, squinting in disbelief. I don't recognize my location, not in the least, because the last time I was conscious, I was upside-down bleeding, trapped in the seat of a burning beauty.

I remember pain and sickness, which are unfamiliar now, as I feel brand new. The only emotion I share between that moment and now is confusion. I keep telling myself to keep my eyes open, but with every passing second, they remain the way they are--closed.

I find my face with my hands, and when my palms reach my brow, they open, wincing from the light breaking through my fingers. I move my hands and take in my new surroundings.

I'm standing in front of a sink. I look up to a large, fogged mirror, the way a mirror gets when you've just had a very long, hot shower. I spin around and with a breath the word "fuck" escapes my lips as I'm in yet another washroom. Spinning back to the large mirror I notice I can see parts of my body reflected back from where the fog had been wiped away.

As I take a step backward, followed by another, until my back touches the stall, I notice these wiped areas are words written, a message left in the fog, it reads,

"There still may be more, so keep an eye out."

I am not simply confused; I'm a combination of irrationality trying to make sense of a senseless situation. I'm not just missing something, I'm missing everything.

I walk back to the mirror and wipe away the message, and when the fog is gone, I'm taken aback by the person who stands in front of me. I'm shaved, washed, and I've got a clean black and white suit on. I open my shirt and loosen my tie.

My wounds have been cleaned and dressed, and with that I look to the sink and notice the empty sterile gauze packages, the metallic bowl with bloody diluted water, the surgical scissors and unused sutures. In the sink next to this is a razor accompanied by a can of shaving cream. I've been cleaned, shaved, and repaired, and all of this happened right here.

But where am I? This washroom isn't the good old diner bathroom; no, this place is professional, bright and posh.

Let's not get overwhelmed with how I got here, no, I need to focus on getting out. The joy of cryptic messages, I smile as I straighten my tie, in the large semi-fogged bathroom mirror that spans over a decadent pearl countertop and corners into a separate mirror right next to the exit.

This is where I see another message scribed into the fog, plastered plainly on the mirror next to the exit, something I couldn't have missed if I had tried.

"Quit trying to figure it out, just leave. Oh, and you're out of ammo. Good luck gorgeous."

I quickly pull my gun from its holster, hidden under my left arm, and with it solidly in my right hand I disengage the clip into my left. Son of a bitch, I'm out, how the fuck did this happen? Wait, oh that's right, it's a waste of time trying to figure that out but stubborn old me pulls at my pockets and at my belt for an extra clip. I don't find any ammo, but I do find that brown cardboard textured envelope half crushed in my pocket.

I pull the envelope out, opening it up, spilling its contents on the expensive surface of the counter, right next to the washroom exit. From it falls a micro-SD card. The SD stands for secure digital; it's a flash memory card that fits into my cell phone, and I'm always impressed at how much information this holds, because the thing is no bigger than a dime.

Into my phone the SD card goes. My phone recognizes it immediately, and into my phone's menu I go, bringing up the memory card screen. It shows me that this SD card contains videos, images, and sound clips.

It's a complete account of the life of the girl I used to love. What she does, where she works, what she does after work, where she lives, even where she goes for fun. Someone wants her dead, but it doesn't explain the claim, or what the policy is. All it says is her policy expired yesterday, and according to this, she was supposed to die, yesterday, at a bar, her favorite bar. She was supposed to be poisoned. It says it was meant to look like a drug overdose, the drug: Rohypnol, the date rape drug.

I shake my head in disgust. Whoever manifested this plan, for wanting her dead, wanting me to enforce that, and wanting me to purposely set it up so she would have Rohypnol in her system, well, they just signed their life away, I promise.

The end truly justifies the means, but when I'm the means, well, I'm not that mean.

Ammo or no ammo, I'm going to stop them, even if I have to beat them all to death, with my metallic companion here. Hell, they made me, so they'll have to deal with me.

Basically, something must've clicked as my hand goes for the door. Whatever they wanted me to do, I didn't, and because of that, they are trying to kill me.

Fine by me, things have returned to normality, and I'm comfortable with this, as long as they don't hurt her, things will be fine. Imagine though, if they hadn't wanted to get rid of her, then I wouldn't remember anything, and if I didn't remember anything, well, they wouldn't have this problem. But they do.

You make your own mess.

I'm again left with the taste of why, washing it around my mouth as I slowly and quietly exit yet another washroom, ready again for war. Into a large hallway, dimly lit by the electrical buzz of halogen, humming its way down. I must be underground somewhere, because there are no windows. This place sounds like a factory; I can hear machines in the distance. A strange chemical smell lingers in the hall, and this hallway seemingly continues on for a distance in both directions from where this washroom is.

At every twenty feet or so there is another hallway branching off elsewhere. I don't even know where I'm going, that is, until I see blood, lingering from under a door about ten feet from me.

It leads me into a room, which appears to be some sort of security station, unguarded. I can't find any corpse, but a small pool of what appears to be human blood coagulates in front of me. This pool begins directly under one of the chairs that sit in front of this massive collection of small security screens. Most of them are turned off, and the tape has been popped out. Behind me to the right is a blinking red light. There is an alarm going off, but I can't hear it. Below that is some sort of electrical box where wires have been gutted out and the box has been broken into.

Searching the room I still don't find the source of the blood, so I go back to the security tape, and I gently push it in, and take a seat listening to it gently rewind. When it finally stops, one of the black screens gains picture, and the next several minutes of tape bring nothing but horror.

There I am, on camera, somewhere else in the building. Glancing from the clock to the time counter on the tape, it indicates this happened an hour ago. But there, in a ten by twelve monitor, an hour ago, walking down these hallways, is me. Shooting people, people I don't recognize, who I can't because the picture isn't clear. At every skip, the camera moves to a different section, a section which I'm ridding of life. I don't remember doing this, but that's me, unloading my guns, changing clips, and emptying them into every single person that I come in to contact with. I don't remember doing this, and I don't know why I would.

I don't like why very much, in fact, when and if I do get answers, I'm going to stop asking why for a long while, as long as I can, because really not knowing is really getting old.

NINE

Deafened by machines, I wander through what I can only assume to be a factory. Knowing my luck with assumptions I'll take a shot in the dark and just say it is what it is.

I don't remember this place and it doesn't hurt when I try, meaning I've never actually been here, so why is it so familiar? Maybe it's the overwhelming pungent chemical stench I'm drowning in, taking a memory from somewhere else I've been. Maybe it's the burning sensation in my nostrils, or maybe what is being processed here, is something I know. It feels as if this smell, the smell of whatever is being processed here, belongs in two different memories. One place for it lies in the past, one belongs in the present, and if I could figure it out, I'd be more aware of the people entering this building from the doors I am attempting to exit from.

I walk down aisles of massive machinery following signs pointing to an exit. As I pass a conveyor belt, I then know what the smell is. Pills, but not just any pills, my pills. The drug that has bound me to the life I now wish to leave. This is where two streets meet. This drug is the same drug I stopped production long ago; maybe not stopped but delayed. As I collect a handful of these little grey and black bastards, I know now I didn't stop it. I just set it back long enough for them to develop something else.

This is how they found me.

My past gains relevance to my present as I begin to pick apart what was back then—those people, the house I blew up—they all have relevance, and that connection is the company. I found this out right before the day at the creek. I was going to do something about it. Turn them in, maybe get revenge like I did with the house, but I've never been to this factory, so how am I here now? I woke up here, that's how. I don't know how I got here, but I am, so while I am, I'll do what I promised and finish what I started.

I need to find the lab; like dominos this place will fall, the lab first and all the pieces drop from there. I'm intending to blow this place up, where and why I ever decided to pick this path for myself becomes unimportant because if these pills can do what they did to me, imagine for a moment what they could do to hundreds of people like me, thousands of people like me. They could switch off populations, if they haven't already.

I've made a list of priorities, first being, do what I have to do now and get out. Second, find Jess and let her know, explain somehow, just tell her I love her, and make sure she's all right. Third, find and execute anyone involved in this company. Fourth, remember everything else.

I know I work for a company posing as a life insurance company, I know I lost my life, I know they made me a new one, and I know I was sent here to kill someone I love. I know if I would have done that, my old life would've become irrecoverable, and any chance of getting it back would be gone. Now I know despite not remembering anything about myself previous to today, somewhere in me, that guy continues to dream of his life, and if we're anything alike, we'll get it back.

I move off the path for the exit heading toward an electronically locked double door. On the side is a mechanism for a swipe card and on the ground in front of the mechanism is a dead security guard with a swipe pass. Convenient or intentional, it works out in my favor. As I pick the pass off the dead guard, I notice in the metallic shine of the door, heavily armed men covered in flat black tactical gear, circling around behind me.

I quickly swipe the magnetic strip, waiting impatiently for the light to go green and as soon as it does, I'm through the door, followed by the sound of suppressed MP5 navy rounds digging into everything around me.

Another hail of bullets avoided, I bound down the hall with no intent of retaliation because I'm completely void of the means to retaliate. I'm not superhuman, these guys all have guns, they all know whom they're shooting at, and they have been properly trained for this moment. Sadly, for me, this exact moment is the moment they intend to put me down.

I scramble into a lab throwing a nearby chair at the door in a meager attempt to slow them down. As I dive behind a large worktable covered in beakers, burners, bottles, and hills of paper, I hear round after round of suppressed machine guns ripping at the table from the doorway, embedding slug after slug into its frame and top, and completely liquefying the solids from atop the table sending the remnants to the concrete below.

The cease of fire comes as no surprise as I hear whispers of warning,

"You want to kill us all? Save your rounds for the target."

I glance around to see pipes snaking from the walls to each of these tables. On every table there are valves protruding from them, a simple set-up for gas to fuel a burner. Every single table is like a bomb waiting to go off. I can hear them slowly entering the room, watching their reflection off the windows; they begin to circle the table I was last seen diving behind. Directly to my right, no more than ten feet away, is a door. I don't know where it leads but as long as it gets me out of this room, I'll take it.

Again, without hesitation I move. I don't stop to open this door; I just break on through it. Two suppressed rounds follow me, one digs into the door, the other shatters the glass in the frame. I don't stop moving; in thoughtless action I begin to knock the valves open. As I charge through another lab, every table, a valve hisses. I bound through three labs before running into a barrier, a single lab worker, completely unaware of the situation, becomes a speed bump in my escape.

I smash into this seemingly unaware scientist, his oversized lab coat trips us, and as we hit the ground, I wrap my forearm around his throat and lift him back to his feet. Through a chocked gurgle, I relax my grip,

"Greyor?"

I continue to move backward, searching blindly with my feet for another door.

"Greyor, you're alive? Well of course you're alive...well this proves it."

"My name is Johnny."

He tries to free himself, but I quickly send my knee to his back, reminding him what's going on.

"Greyor listen to me, we don't have much time. I'm not your enemy. Whoever is after you, I can talk to them, let me talk to them. You're too valuable."

I continue to drag him through what seems to be an endless journey, lab after lab I tug him closer to the tables spinning more valves open. Every room I leave is quickly filled by invisible liquid petroleum gas.

"What're you doing?" "What does it look like?"

I back through another lab door, and this time I'm greeted by a new image. An open hallway, and at the end of this hallway, double doors with small square windows and darkness glaring from behind them.

Quickly, with one hand, I rip my pack of cigarettes and my lighter from my pocket, pulling my last cigarette from the pack. I throw it between my lips; walking backwards I light its end.

"Greyor, you can't smoke here."

I tighten my grip on his neck and take a deep breath of carbon monoxide. Time seems to disappear as I stare at the door from which I came. Slowly walking back toward the double doors, I pull at the cigarette again, watching red burn through the grey and black. The smoke lingers between my lips before I finally inhale it down. As my back touches the double doors, the hermetically sealed double doors, doors that cause this hallway to become like a wind tunnel when they are opened and closed, pulling the air out of the hallway briefly until sealed again. I drop the cigarette to the side; make sure it's still ablaze. I release my grip momentarily on the scientist,

"Open it."

He swipes his pass and within moments, a sound of a lock disengaging forces me backward, as the doors swing open to the night. I pull him back, walking carefully and quickly down large metal stairs into a parking lot full of eighteen- wheelers, cube vans, company and civilian cars alike. I enter yet another maze, with the same intention as always, to leave. As we leave the staircase and sluggishly make our way through the cars, one word, which means nothing to me, comes as an order from the top of staircase we just came from,

"Stop."

I spin around with the scientist as my shield, looking up at my five heavily armed pursuers and at this moment, five red dots are deckled on us moving within centimeters of each other. Before I'm given the opportunity to retort, the scientist cuts me off,

"I want you to disengage. You must know who I am, so, you're going to turn around and let us leave. He's too important to be killed now. I'll talk to him."

"Yeah, buddy it isn't going to matter soon,"

I smile, while the scientist half looks back at me and then looks back to the men in tactical gear who still haven't moved, themselves or their sights.

I pull the scientist as I start to walk backwards. I watch as they bring one eye closed with the intention to mow us down, with a final word their fingers begin to squeeze backward but before the guns go off, light breaks into night as fire tears from behind them, followed by glass, metal, wood, stone, and finally the sound of a building being incinerated.

The windows shatter simultaneously as they first appear to fall inward and then they're guided out like bullets from a gun. With the glass come window frames of metal and wood splintering away, tearing with them the surrounding stone, and not just the stone of the building but the asphalt surrounding it. All of it embraces this change, guided by fire and force, followed by explosion after explosion. The first row of cars, trucks and vans are punched backward, soaring into other parked vehicles. Everything seems to grow louder and stronger.

I'm not walking backwards anymore, I'm gasping for air, protruding from a wind shield of a parked company car that I was thrown into. For the second time today I'm winded, and to make things worse, I can barely hear anything but ringing. This isn't just in my head; I've been deafened by the blast, and I fight to tear myself free from the shattered glass with the least possible bodily harm. As I get up on the hood to gauge the damage I've caused, the vertigo kicks in from inner ear imbalance and I fall, sliding off the hood like a cop in a cheesy chase scene.

Thankfully I can stand. Barely, but I can, and I begin to laugh uncontrollably as a sentence tip- toes across my psyche...

Smoking really can kill you.

I look around the dilapidated parking lot while stuffing my finger in my ear and wiggling it, in the attempt to regain my hearing. I can't hear my own voice as I bark obscenities. I try to listen. I focus on the sound of the consequential explosions; the fire tearing into places where it wasn't moments ago, gasoline ignites inside trapped lines and tanks of vehicles that are ablaze. Fire tears free from solid earth and stone as if hell was coming for a visit. It smothers out sound and the ringing in my ears stops. I stumble over something, suddenly realizing I've just tripped over the injured scientist. I kneel and inspect his damage. He only appears to be mildly injured, very little wounds, with very little glass embedded in them. Scrapes and bruises but nothing appears to be serious. I shake him, trying to bring him back to consciousness. When his eyes open, he blinks at me.

"Am I dead?" "No."

"What happened?"

He sits up, staring at what's left of the building.

His jaw drops slightly as he looks back at me. "Why did you do that?"

"Because that building produces the drug that's kept me away, that's why."

"Greyor, you don't understand."

"Stop fucking calling me Greyor, my name is Johnny."

"Alright then, Johnny, listen. You are a living wonder. You really have no memory of Greyor?"

"Buddy, I can barely remember anything about myself. When I do, I'll try and remember Greyor." "No matter, which is amazing, you are the only case of regaining cognitive control after being exposed to that medication, which makes you— just as I previously assumed—special. If you have a concept of a life previous to the one you assumed after medication trials began, then you are the only subject in which complete cognitive failure didn't occur when the chemicals were removed. Fascinating..."

I grab him by the collar, lift him to his feet, and charge him into a nearby van. I turn his attention to the explosion and then refocus him on me.

"Wake up man, look around, does this look fascinating? People are trying to kill me, alright; there is nothing fascinating about that. They took my life, my love, and left me broken. To top things off, I don't even know who the fuck I am, so, if you wouldn't mind, I'm due an explanation or at least some goddamn sympathy."

I release him. He stands there expressionless for a moment. He looks at a loss for words, but without wasting his face loses interest and he becomes human momentarily,

"I'm sorry Johnny, I can only imagine how confused you are. Let me explain, come, I'll get you out of here. I know you don't trust me, but you have to hear what I've got to say."

I look around and witness my resolve, more collateral damage in my war for awareness. He's right, I don't trust him, but I've run out of options. I look at the burning rubble of a once-mighty pharmaceutical factory, one I brought down, praying it was the right choice, and I know this path will continue, bringing the same result. A road left open is a road yet to be taken, and I have no other choice but to go with this guy.

I step back, making way for him to move. My eyes don't move off him as he leads me to the back of what's left of this parking lot.

He wanders up to a tan civic. Rust litters the doors and wheel wells, and the trunk hangs ajar. I raise my eyebrow as he turns to look at me, he motions with a nod for me to get in the passenger seat, as I come around the car, he finally gets his door open.

Jumping in, he pops the passenger side door open. Right before I get in, flashing lights illuminate the horizon, red and bright, loud and fast, fire trucks speed in our direction. I sit down shaking my head, knowing it's too late, but at least somebody is coming,

"Let's go."

THE EXPLANATION

He takes me to his lab at the university he teaches at. Let me rephrase that, he says he teaches here. I still don't know if trust is something I'm ready to hand out. In a small but comfortable office we sit. He asks me to make myself comfortable, but I shake my head with a smile and a sigh.

"I'll try and keep this as simple as possible. Once the medication is introduced into the system, it causes the test subject to regress mentally. Not their intelligence, but their memory. Imagine your memories written down on a chalkboard, the medication is an eraser, and it just wipes away everything. Mind you, like the chalkboard, if you look closely enough, you can see something that had been previously written. I guess in your case, somehow, you were able to decipher that.

Every physical memory is there, but identity, that's the target. The identity of the subject is gone. In your case Johnny, it was different, because you started the medication in the hospital, after your surgery,"

"My surgery? Tell me more about my surgery."

"When I first met you, you had been shot in the head. You underwent a surgery that I oversaw, I didn't perform it, but I was there. I don't know exactly what was done but that was the beginning. It was the start of your transformation, and it wasn't the last time you were in surgery. Johnny,

you have no idea how lucky you are to be alive."

"Lucky? People keep telling me how lucky I

am, lucky to be alive, lucky to remember what I do, or should I say, what little I do."

"How you remember, that's the mystery because the others couldn't remember anything before the medication once it had left their system. They became mostly catatonic. Just vessels to an empty mind, repeating echoes of what little they could reach for, and in the end, without the medication, they'd just shut down. Somehow, you didn't, and I can only assume it's because of your condition."

"My condition? What do you mean my condition; I have a condition now?"

"Johnny, you've always had it, fight or flight.

You feel it right now, don't you?"

I may not know exactly what he's talking about, but he's right, there is something else, something that never quite fits, that's starting to.

"So, what now?"

"Before entering the medication into your system, right after your surgery, we discovered you to have a constant release of epinephrine in your blood, as if you were constantly in danger, ready to fight, or ready to run. It was amazing, when testing that theory, to assure that it truly was constant. We ran blood test after blood test, and you always had exceedingly high levels in your blood."

"How do you know it's constant? I mean how do you know you really know? Maybe it could be because I got shot in the fucking head. Maybe it's because I couldn't remember anything and instinctually, I knew I was in danger – ever think of that?"

"That's a good theory Johnny, it really is... but we tested that. Your normal epinephrine levels were that of a person in a life-threatening situation even when you were asleep, even when we induced unconsciousness..."

"Induced unconsciousness? What the fuck?" "We knocked you out, using sedatives. Now,

after subjecting you to a situation that could provoke your life to feel threatened, well, your epinephrine levels should have caused your heart to explode."

I'm confused as ever, but interested, because all of this can explain why I'm still alive, and why others are dying in the attempt to stop me.

"How long has it been since you took your medication?"

"A while, almost ten hours give or take…How do you sleep, knowing what you do to people?"

"I don't really have a choice, plus, I'm a scientist Johnny, everything has a price, especially the accomplishment of great things. I mean, originally, I designed this chemical to fight the effects of frontotemporal dementia and Alzheimer's, but when the side effect was memory loss, the company approached me. They funded me my experiments, provided I continued to reinforce the side effects, and made sure the drug produced that effect."

"The cure really is worse than disease, isn't it?"
"Sadly Johnny, it is."

"So, what now, I mean, can you help me?" "Johnny, I don't know how, I've been looking

for a way to conquer memory loss and all I've done is create a medication that promotes it. I don't think you want any more of my help."

"Ok, how about your name?"

"Henry Alrick. It's on the door Johnny."

I look at the lab door and there in black Times New Roman lettering is his name backwards through the glass pane.

"How do you feel?"

"Sick. I've felt horrible all day, and not just because I'm remembering the life I lost, but I think about the people trying to kill me, and losing a lot of blood might be a factor. Listen Henry, do you have any idea of who you're working for?"

He looks to the ground and sighs before meeting my eyes again.

"Some."

"Do you know about the insurance? The cover? Where they get all that money to pay you?" "Some."

"What do you know Henry?"

"I know that you used to be, and now are again, Johnny Valentyne. Who, through extensive brain damage, memory loss, cognitive re-education, living a new identity for several years, and plastic surgery has somehow returned to an identity that a company and a drug tried so hard to erase. I don't know how you do it, and continue to do it, how messed up you should be. You seem to survive off impulse. I do know you were Greyor Allblack that worked for the company, just recently failing to follow through on a job, and disappearing.

I know this because I was warned you may be after me. But I must know, Johnny, do you have any idea of the company you're working for?"

"I know enough. What I need you to do is either tell me I stopped the production of that medication or let me know how I can."

He looks at me with an expression full of something that isn't sympathy. Maybe it's disbelief, maybe it's compassion, or maybe he knows something that he can't tell me. Whatever it is, it doesn't matter because the one person I want, is the one person that has repeatedly tried to kill me and failed. I can't seem to kill him, and somewhere right now, he's waiting for me to try again.

We discuss the cost and the risk.

We spend time discussing science. Science, he tells me, science is risk. Discovering anything worth discovering is apparently worth the risk. No endeavor is easy. Nothing ever is, and if it is, I'm told it's not worth a thing.

He could be right but where does that leave us, him and I?

I can't kill him because he's a pawn. He didn't do this to me intentionally.

But if he lives, well if he lives, so does the drug.

I look at him, but he appears distracted. Like me, he's elsewhere in his head, no longer a part of this would-be conversation.

"Johnny?"

He comes out of the haze and stares up at me struggling to lift his head.

"Johnny, you know with me still here, they'll just rebuild."

"I know Henry. With or without you they'll make more."

"The formula is incomplete, severely incomplete. It was the only way I knew for sure they would still need me. With me here, they'll make more, and I'll help them."

He turns away, shaking his head, trying to pull himself up and away from the overwhelming dark that reaches for his psyche, replacing reason with blame.

He turns with tears welling in his eyes and his voice grinds out an octave higher.

"Why not? Why shouldn't you, I deserve it. I've spent the last eight years helping people lose their memory. The absolute opposite of what I originally set out to do."

"I know that feeling..." He cuts me off.

"No, Johnny, you don't. You didn't consciously choose to sabotage your life. That damage was forced on you, and I helped enforce it."

"That's one way of looking at it, but you can figure out a way to undo the effects. Just make another drug Henry, it may take time, but hell – you have all the time you need; you'll be unemployed soon."

I chuckle, trying to remove myself momentarily, because I can't stand to watch this guy fall apart. I haven't felt like this in – well, to be honest, I don't remember the last time I've felt like this and it's overwhelming.

"No, Johnny those effects cannot be undone by another medication. I've tried, Johnny. Everything I've tried has just made things worse. Much, much worse."

I don't move.

He sits up from silence, staring at nothing in particular. His eyes simply graze off corners of each table, bouncing side to side. Examining, he looks from the table, calculating distance from here to there. He looks at the exits, the doors around him, how many are there, which is the closest and he thinks about running, but then he just looks back at me. "Your gun."

Extending his palm like a hungry child, expecting me to feed him, and the request turns to command.

"Valentyne, give me your gun."

"Henry."

I don't move, I don't blink, and I don't breathe. "Please."

In one quick motion my gun is cocked, hammer engaged, barrel pointing in a seemingly harmless direction, and my gun is now in his hand.

"Thank you."

"Henry, don't be stupid."

"Well, what the fuck am I supposed to be Johnny? Eight years, eight goddamn years doing everything, everything, fucking absolutely everything backward. I'm going the wrong fucking way, and I know there is just more guilt, sickness, and mistakes waiting there for me. I have undone any chance at decreasing, maybe even eliminating, early memory..."

He chokes up, his throat clenches his voice box, and his sentence ends with a sigh.

"...loss and now, now I have no choice, if I live..."

He chokes again.

"… If I live, they'll make me make more and I can't Johnny, I can't do that anymore. I mean, now that I've met you. I mean, you don't get to come face to face with your mistakes very often and to have them feel sorry for you…"

He looks up with tears welling under his lids as he tries to shake them away. Shaking his five o'clock cheeks but the tears run slowly down the sides of his nose. He looks up at the ceiling as his arm slowly rises with gun in hand. Limply, he slides the barrel up against his temple.

"Henry."

I try to get his attention.

Henry takes an almost endless breath, inhaling until his eyebrows look like the wingspan of a bird. His chest rises to the point where it looks like it'll explode out and upward.

I don't move.

His eyes lock shut as he makes his final exhale outward, the long-winded, greatly anticipated exhale and with it a single tear glides down his cheek and rolls under his chin.

His face finds its final expression in the form of a wince as he squeezes the trigger.

Click.

The hammer thrusts a pin nowhere before snapping back.

Surprise as his eyes open and he's greeted by my unimpressed expression.

"Fucking hell Henry."

"It's empty?"

"Of course it's empty. Why would I hand my gun, a loaded gun, to someone in your state?"

His eyes widen.

"It's fucking empty."

His eyes open wider, welling with water.

"You son of a…" I cut him off. "Henry."

"Well, what am I going to do then?"

"Fix it."

"I told you, I can't."

"Try."

"I can't."

His eyes trail off as does his mind, wandering through his thoughts from idea to idea and then suddenly the tears stop, his expression calms, and he stares back at me. Maybe there isn't anything he can do. He confirms it, once, twice, a third time even.

Nothing he can do.

That sentence repeats in my head, again and again until he looks up at me with the same look, he gave me when he accepted my gun.

"Give me your medication." "Do you ever say please?"

"Johnny, please just give me your medication."

"Why? What the hell are you going to do with it?"

I already have some idea as to what he's going to do with it, but I rummage through my pockets anyway.

"It's the only way."

"Only way, what's the only way?" "So, they can't make me make more."

"It's called free will Henry. It's fun, you should indulge once in a while, make some of your own decisions."

"Jesus Johnny, are you ever serious? Come on, they'll torture me until I break, they'll make me."

I hand him the bottle full of those little grey and black pills. As he opens it, he looks up at me as if it's the last time he'll see me and he's probably right.

"There has to be something else you can do Henry."

"There isn't Johnny. I'm sorry."

I sigh, shaking my head as he throws back the bottle, swallowing two pills. He puts the bottle down as I walk for the door.

"Johnny?"

I stop and turn around to look at him. "Yeah?"

"Thank you." "For?" "Forgiving me."

As I turn, he begins to sweat, staring off and out into the darkness.

I walk down the dimly lit staircase of his building, chuckling because as it turns out, some people really do get a taste of their own medicine.

TEN AND A HALF

After ditching Henry's car in a corn field not far from my next destination I can't shake the feeling that no matter what happens next—mind you that's if next will ever come—that no matter what I do, there will be more blood. If there is, let's hope it's not hers, or mine.

Trying to connect my memories to make sense gets easier as every minute passes, especially now that I'm trekking through a field because there's really not much else to do but think.

Think back, but how far? Because I really can't reach for anything before the last hour of my normal life before I dug those graves, before I came home to find Laurie, before I saved Jess from the house I blew up, and before I blew myself up. Before that day everything is still a haze but hopefully in time everything will systematically fall back into place, or at least I hope it does. Because right now I function off the idea that there is a garage out on one of these farms that belongs to me, or at least what's left of me here.

In awe, I leave the seemingly endless field out and on to and open grass lawn. The lawn leads to a dark farmhouse and connected to that farmhouse is a garage, a garage I remember.

It sparks memories; this familiar garage brings me back to my youth, before the city and before the shit.

This is Max's family's farm, or at least it was a long time ago.

Max was my best friend growing up and he still was right before I died, but I can't remember much of my life and that means I don't think I'd remember much of Max, other than that I grew up with him. As I ramble on mentally, I'm almost at the garage, and somehow, I've overlooked something.

The eighteen-wheeler parked in the laneway... I don't remember if Max wanted to become a truck driver, then again, I wonder if anyone's even home. If they are, they probably wouldn't appreciate some guy going through their dead loved one's stuff.

The house is dark, and the only sounds are from an engine clicking away as it contracts with the cool night air. The night is silent with the exception of the cooling engine and the insects that buzz monotonously somewhere in the dark. I make every attempt to stay vigilant because I don't want a repeat of the rest of my day. Constantly watching over my shoulder is a bitter feeling I wish I could do without.

With every step and effort to be silent, I cross the yard and head around to the back entrance of the garage. When I get around to the front, I sigh, because of course a very large padlock locks the garage, and no, the key isn't resting comfortably in it, waiting to be turned.

I look around for any hiding spots.

The mat in front of the side door here…nothing.

Or maybe in one of the many plant pots littering the ground around the garage…. nothing

Or in the barrels and buckets or amongst the gravel of the makeshift driveway…nothing

Or under those stupid fucking lawn gnomes littering the lawn, causally staring at every move I make…nope…nothing.

More memory, trying to find the correct memory, I close my eyes and try and remember this place and I do just that, I remember.

As I turn and open my eyes there in the dark is an old tree and in the middle of the old tree is a hole dug out with time and maybe with the help of an animal. That's where the key is going to be.

I walk over and reach into it and after minutes of searching blindly, I feel something metallic. From the hole I pull a dirty gold-colored key. It's teeth rugged and aged but still intact, it feels familiar because I've used this key numerous times that even if I wanted to, I couldn't remember how many times I've opened that garage.

I walk back to the garage, stop and look around for any changes to my surroundings. Any lights that are on that weren't on moments ago, anything new that wasn't previously there. When I finally feel comfortable, I jam the key into the lock. After several rough tries and several wrist-cracking jerks I manage to spring the old lock, and it pops open. I remove the lock, letting it hang and begin to gently lift the garage door as slowly and quietly as possible.

Even with my best efforts, the sound that this garage is making makes it impossible to make its ascent any quieter. So, I repeat the same process before throwing it completely open, look around for any changes and when nothing's changed, I let the garage finish its ascent on its own.

The garage opens with a screeching metallic smash, the kind of sound you get when you haven't opened it in years, the kind of sound you get when rain, snow, and the rest of the corroding elements have gone to town on it. Beyond the mouth of the garage is darkness, dust and cob- webs.

I dig my Zippo from the depths of my pocket and flick it open. After several annoying skin- tearing turns the wick ignites, and not more than five feet in front of me is the maw of a dusty black car. Not just any dusty, dirty, debris-covered car but my dusty, dirty, debris-covered carbon black Monte Carlo. It hasn't been moved in ages, but the tires are still inflated.

Thankfully, and I mean this, the elements have been kind to my car. I walk to the driver's side and slowly inspect the condition of its body, and that's when something smacks me right in the left eye. I shake my head, wipe a tear, and bring the Zippo to the direction where I got struck, and there dangling in the musty air, is the cord to the light above me, covered in webs. I laugh as I pull at it, and to my surprise, artificial light burns my pupils into pins.

"Fuck."

I whisper to myself, smiling, staring at the ground, and I notice something off. Another set of footprints, smaller footprints, more recent footprints, and my hand is already on my gun. I raise my sight, leveling it with the driver's side window, across its dirty surface, a handprint that's been smeared from the border to the middle of the window. Not the whole hand, just the fingertips. Cautiously, I approach the sweet end of my

1984 Monte Carlo super sport. On the rear window, letters are written across the dirty surface,

"Wash me Johnny, I'm dirty."

The handwriting is done with bubble letter font. Each letter seems more feminine than masculine, curving gracefully into one and another, surrounded by scribbled hearts, X's and O's. As my eyes scan these dirty sentences I actually—and I really don't understand how—but I feel sad. Not just sad, but sad and lonely. I sigh, as I pull my hair from my forehead, bunching it into a mess and then scratching it.

I'm mesmerized by this message.

The message she wrote. The message on the driver's side window of the car I've driven a grand total of ten times and now I have no idea if she's in trouble or not. I have to get to her before anyone else does. All the while, I'm here staring at my old car, in this garage, in the middle of nowhere.

I open the driver's side door as my expression goes blank because I feel the cold barrel of a shotgun press against my temple.

"Very bad move buddy."

"Fuck, I do not have time for this."

I gaze from my peripherals and there, holding a shotgun, is a sour-looking Max coldly staring at me, looking like at any moment, he's about to repaint my car with my brains.

"Oh, I'm sorry I didn't know car thieves had fucking time constraints."

He roughly shoves me with the barrel,

"Take it easy Max. Last I checked this car belongs to me."

His expression grows worse as he isn't amused at what he believes to be a lie.

"Listen Max, really, I would love to explain how I'm alive and why my face is different, but man, I just don't have the fucking time."

He looks at me and his expression canvases confusion, anger, and disgust and it appears at any moment he's ready to pull that trigger.

"Max, get fucked, I do not have time..."

I laugh

"...You're looking pretty good for a girl."

The shaved head, shotgun-wielding monster relaxes his grip on the gun and the barrel slides from its place as I let out a heavy sigh. With tears in his eyes he relaxes, studying me, his expression paints impossibility.

"Johnny?"

I nod, smiling.

Saving myself with memories through slogans and sayings never gets old.

He drops the shotgun and picks me up into a bear hug as his voice leaves the threatening stature it once had for a lighter, happier tone. As he crushes my ribs he begins to scream,

"Manny! Manny, get your ass out here, you're never going to believe this, Manny!"

Max pulls me from the garage toward the house and when we get to the porch outside the kitchen, Manny is standing in the doorway. His head is cocked to the right, his eyes tired, and he looks confused. He's trying to figure out where he knows me from, and with a single nod and feigned word from his lips as he says my name without sound a tear rolls down his cheek as he lunges at me.

I sit up on a sturdy rocking chair, parked in front of an ancient table in an old kitchen that looks almost exactly how it looked the last time I was here, except the three that usually sat at it. With time they've changed. Yes, some more than others but the comfort is still there, the friendship unchanged. The kind of friendship where silence can tell a story. With friends like these, you can have a whole conversation without speaking, but not this time. This time, I explain.

In front of me, a steaming cup of coffee and with the coffee, the kind of comfort that you find in years of friendship where sometimes the shortest story sums up more than a long winded, unnecessarily complex play by play of the life and resurrection of their friend. My memories return, more and more with every minute, and I know I don't have long.

They both keep smiling, looking from each other to me, and shake their heads almost in unison, both in disbelief about who I am and where I've been. I interrupt the moment with a surely annoying question,

"Does Manny live with you Max?" "No, he just crashed here, got in late."

Manny laughs, he starts to speak but goes silent because, suddenly, something makes me jump as I

realize my phone is vibrating in my pocket and before I can reach it, it stops vibrating and begins to ring loudly, continuously synthesizing the same ring over and over again until finally I free my phone and slide it open to my ear.

"Hello."

I speak into silence but from the silence, a muffled exhale and then a voice that sends shivers through me.

"Hello John, how've you been? It seems you've gone home."

"What do you want?"

"You know what I want. But what do you want John? I can guess. Do you want me to guess? Oh wait, that's right, why guess when I know. Because you want her and she's with me."

From the phone, I hear a muffled shriek and the sounds of struggle.

"Sorry about that John but she can't come to the phone. If you want her let's, make a trade, sound good?"

"I swear, Sketch if you touch her, I'll..."

Without control, overwhelmed, I scream into the speaker and then I quickly bite my tongue, realizing anger is pointless.

"Kill me, John? Don't worry; if you accept my offer, she lives."

"What do you want?"

"Your life for hers. Simple enough, isn't it? It's every cliché one can only dream of, right, John?"

"Where are you?"

"Your house, John. Come home before I make it mine."

The dial tone of my phone is two beeps, signifying the call has ended.

Both Manny and Max stayed absolutely silent, listening intently to that conversation, if you can call it a conversation. Concern runs down each cheek and with a wince they both rise simultaneously, awaiting my action.

I try to explain what's going on but before I even get to finish my first sentence, they're helping me to the door.

We all walk from Max's house to the car waiting for me in the dimly lit garage.

"What're you going to do?" Max smiles.

"Save her and kill him." "Anything we can do?" "I can't involve you."

"It's too late for that Johnny."

"I know, but I need to do this alone."

"You said that last time and look what happened."

"Good point but just be there before the cops get there."

"Always are, just like last time, eh Manny?" Manny smiles and then nods.

He makes gesture for an explosion. "Ah right. Makes sense now" "Does it?"

"Not really Max, and I don't know when it will make sense again."

"Johnny we can help man; you don't have to go this alone."

"I do, just one more time. This time, I'm going to get it right."

I reach the Monte Carlo's door.

"Is the last time we're going to see you bud?" "I doubt it."

"If we don't?" "Take care of her."

"Always do man, we always do."

Manny speaks up from his speechless phase, "Johnny, I missed you man. It's good to see you."

"You too Manny. You too."

I step from the driver's side door and throw my arms around their shoulders and hug them. I'm almost back now, I can feel my humanity return with the help of my friends, and now I just have to get her back. With a little time, everything should return to whatever state of life I used to call normal. At least, I can only hope.

TO KILL A BASTARD

Know your enemy. If you are going to learn anything about combat that is what you need to know first and foremost. Knowledge succeeds victory nine out of ten times. If you know what you're getting yourself into, then you are more likely to come out standing. It doesn't matter what the cause, because if you seek to overcome the odds and I mean any odds, know exactly what you're up against and if you don't, well you're walking into loss and some things, well some things you can't afford to lose like your life or the lives of the people you love.

It took me about half an hour driving at a speed that would easily be considered unnecessary under any other circumstances to get to my old house. I'm a block away, and my house is just around the corner.

I need to see Sketch before he sees me, and considering my past with him, it feels nearly impossible. But he's expecting the man he built, trained, and unleashed. What he's not expecting is that kid from the hospital bed who spat in his face. He's assuming that I'll sneak in cold and quiet, come in the back, try and sneak up on him, try to follow my training, but that's just what he'll be assuming, and you know what I think of assumptions. Like I said, know your enemy.

I'm running on empty.

My car is running low on gas, my guns without bullets, without jackets, and they're cold.

I struggle to keep my eyes open, my blood pumping, and my heart racing just long enough to finish this.

Before I pull into the long stretch of road leading up to my house, I throw the car in neutral and turn off the headlights, letting the car roll in the shadows of the street. I dig my cell phone out and call the last number that called me. That last number is Sketch's.

One ring slowly hums on to the second and then the second eventually becomes the third and I count on. I focus on the front window of my house, through the blinds. I look for signs of movement. One footrests on the clutch while my other waits for the gas. One hand holds the wheel as I press the phone between my shoulder and ear while my other hand rests on the gear shifter, waiting for an answer.

"Hello John."

His rasp through the microphone is followed immediately by the sound of bullets disintegrating the glass of the window of my house, and then the windshield of my car. With that, my car finds first as I rev it red, the tires catch the asphalt and my car lunges forward furiously.

I'm deafened by the engine and blinded by crumbling glass as my car is now in second gear, red lining and hurdling within seconds from the wall on the front of my house, the wall under the window, the window he stands at, firing round after round at me. Punching from the barrel, bullet after bullet is followed by a silenced hiss.

I hear a bullet knock into the hood of my car as another rips through the seat right behind my head and then I feel a bullet burn through me as I find third gear. Time stops as does my car as it punctures through the wall and window, crumbling the front part of my house down around my car's back end as it enters my old living room. From within all the chaos, through the exploding furniture, the falling glass, and behind the raining wood and stone I see Sketch firing blindly into the driver's side of my car as he slams against the hood, and my car doesn't stop until it hits the wall behind him.

He's pinned between the obliterated front end of my Monte Carlo and the shattered wall and cracked foundation, but he still moves, writhing in pain trying to free himself. Before I can get my seat belt off, he squeezes out two more suppressed rounds.

The first runs along my cheek and removes a chunk of my ear before embedding into the speaker behind the back seat. Because of that extremely painful wound, my body contorts downward and the second-round misses, tearing through my steering wheel as I fall out of my car, releasing my seat belt.

I'm on all fours trying to shake the pain, deafened by the sound of my engine roaring, feeding off the gas being fed to it by a broken accelerator. I shake all of it off, my car, the pain, and Sketch screaming, distracting myself long enough to find her and get her out of here. I fight the fear as I look around before standing up. I know she wasn't near him when he started firing because he needed to see me, and he needed me to see her. To distract me so that when I walked in that house the first thing, I would see is...

I look up and sitting there, strapped to a chair in the kitchen, down the hall from the front door in plain view, she's there.

What he didn't anticipate was me driving my car right through the living room and impaling him to the wall, no, he didn't see that coming because now I have the bastard pinned. Like I said, know your enemy.

I stand up with a sigh and a smile as I limp toward the kitchen. I can hear him screaming at me, but I don't listen. I hear him fire off his last round into the kitchen doorway.

I kneel in front of her, gently moving her hair off her face. She's quietly breathing, calm and peaceful with a small abrasion on her eyebrow. For the second time in my life, I'm rescuing her while she's unconscious and despite my damage all I do is smile through the searing pain that riddles my system.

I remove the bonds and lift her, gently cradling her into my chest as I walk down the hallway and out the front door.

I stand on the dimly lit porch, searching around for a safe place. History seems to repeat itself, trapped between now and then, things may be different but every instance here was just like it was back then, or it feels that way, because across the street in front of a house, a small bed of flowers still lives, and I limp toward it. I look down at her and I smile.

Unconsciously, she nestles up against my chest and what appears to be a smile begins to creep across her face. She has no idea what's going on, no idea that I'm here, and I'm carrying her again to a flowerbed, to safety. It appears she feels safe and for a moment, a moment I've waited for even when I didn't know I was waiting for it, I find comfort.

A feeling I can only explain as alien, its warmth gives me strength as I'm almost at the bed of flowers. Unknowingly, I've walked right in front of the window of the living room, and without a moment passing from the time I've stepped out into his view, I hear a suppresser squeeze out several rounds, shrieking through the air, and I feel them dig into my back as I stumble to my right knee.

As I hear them fly by me, I see the bullets turn solid objects like streetlights, plant pottery, wood fences, and even some unfortunate lawn gnomes into debris. With the pain, with the blood, even with my new buried little friends searing in my skin, I stand back up and finish my path. Dirt is thrown up as bullets hail around me, ripping sod chunks from the ground.

When I finally arrive at the bed of flowers, I go back to my knees and gently lay her down. I move her hair away from her face again and I kiss her, the moment that all this has been for.

As I taste her, I'm overwhelmed by a feeling that has kept me alive this entire time, since the first day this began; a feeling I'll hold. A feeling no one, or thing, can take from me. They never could – not the company, not the money, not the pills, and no, not even Sketch because this entire time I've felt this, this love, and it brought me here without me even knowing. The man I was didn't die, he was just trapped between death, drugs and dollars.

As I stand, tears don't just well but run without control. It's not sadness. It's contentment. In my eyes, in my expression, written on my face is serenity and finally with this peace I turn back to the house as history writes what must be done. I stumble and limp toward my shooter, Sketch, who still fights for freedom. Even with how much internal damage he must have sustained, somehow, he still breathes but I promise, he won't for very much longer.

He digs into his mangled lower half for another clip as he painfully tries to pull himself free and then he looks back up to me, limping toward him in the orange glow of the street.

I pull my hair from my forehead and as I feel the cold night breeze cut across its shined surface, I know his end. I reach into the depths of my pocket and feel the cold of my Zippo reach up to greet my fingers. Removing it, I continue, rolling it in my hands, walking on. Somehow, he manages to get the clip into the gun. With a flick of the lid my thumb goes on the abrasive wheel as I hear more suppressed rounds fire out in a panic.

His aim is absent as he too now knows what's coming, because with all the fighting, his lungs draw breath from his mouth and nostrils and now he can smell the gas that fills the living room as my car bleeds out.

As the first bullet punches through my chest, clean through, from front to back, he screams, as he tries to empty round after round in me, to put me down, but I don't fall. As the hot metal breaks through me, I stumble and stagger, but I do not fall as my blood litters the asphalt.

With a flick of my thumb, I create fire, and I stare up at him and I smile in the flickering light of the flame.

With the last of my strength, I toss my Zippo under the car as I fall to my knees never breaking my stare with Sketch and my flame, enjoying the expression that paints his face. With that I focus intently as the metal case skids from the pavement, clinking with every bounce. The flame licks viciously away as if laughing at the wind and motion and how they do little to extinguish it, and I can't help but stare. Not even when I hear the sick sound of something crack as he makes a final attempt to escape.

My Zippo skips like a stone over water bouncing from the asphalt before disappearing under the back end of my poor Monte Carlo. I don't see fire this time and I'm not tossed back like a rag doll in an explosion. I hear laughing, because nothing has happened. I look up at Sketch as he has managed to get one mauled leg from the car, and I watch paralyzed as he feeds his gun yet another clip. He smiles and takes aim.

"Ah, come on," I whisper.

I close my eyes as I hear the hammer go back as his sight is locked perfectly to my skull but then I feel the temperature change, the breeze disappears, and so does he, as heat escapes from below my car. My eyes open as I watch light lick from underneath and catch him, within seconds it engulfs the front end and a split second later the back end is an inferno.

He drops his gun swatting at the fire, but it doesn't stop, it just keeps eating, my car's paint begins to bubble, crack, and finally peel. Then the surrounding crumbled walls and littered floor ignite. In the blink of an eye, fire lights the night and the whole house is burning along with my car and with my car burning, Sketch's guttural cries consume him as does the inferno.

I'm kneeling about fifteen feet from this, from the fire, from the heat and from the sick smell of cooking flesh. The night silence stripped and drowned by the roar of screams and sirens, but these sirens will come too late to save him.

I watch as flesh is stripped from him as his clothes ignite. I watch as the pain washes clean his face and I watch as his hair disappears, and I smile. In a blink of an eye my Monte Carlo fractures as the engine erupts outward and the hood rips into his jaw, tearing his head from his shoulders, decapitating him as the rest of the car shatters. The rogue pieces, doors, glass, frame, become shrapnel annihilating the foundation, the walls, hallway, and rooms which collapse as the house begins to cradle inward, pushing an opaque cloud that screens out the stars littered with burning ember.

Sketch disappears in the collapsing ruin. And that is how to kill a bastard.

END OF THE SWITCH

My eyes open in a daze as I begin to regain a conscious consciousness, the kind of clarity you receive after waking from being unconscious for several hours, the kind that follows a surgery in which bullet fragments and shrapnel were removed in efforts to keep you breathing and those efforts apparently paid off. I guess that's the difference between a .45 caliber bullet and a suppressed 9mm; with one, you have little chance of survival regardless of where the bullet is placed, while the other is shot-place dependent, the 9mm can come out clean while the .45 breaks bones.

That's why I use a .45, the difference between life and death. It doesn't matter if the 9mm has better range and better accuracy. What happens when you're pinned against a wall by a car, you can't really place your shots with that 9mm, and so if you do get a shot in, you hope it hits something vital but if you'd been using the .45 caliber then I'd most likely be dead. Sorry Sketch, it looks like I win that argument.

I'm sitting up in a hospital bed. The morning sun slips in through the shades and warms away the paleness of my room. But within moments it's stolen by clouds, bringing back the dark and artificial light. With awareness comes pain, the pain from several wounds, wounds now sutured closed. I become uncomfortable because I know I'm not alone. I blink several times and in relief I see several cops are sitting in my room staring at me.

"Well hello Mr. Valentyne, welcome back to the land of the living."

"Thanks, I think...Hey, can I have some water?"

One of the larger officers walks over to a small tray and pours a glass from a see-through jug. I hear ice clink together as it falls, bouncing from side to side over the rim. He brings the glass toward me and extends it. I go to take it, but I realize as my hand doesn't even get a foot from my bed because I'm handcuffed to it,

"Little help?"

He shakes his head and makes motions for me to take a drink from the glass with his help. I sigh and take back a couple of gulps before nodding that I'm done.

"So, you've got a lot to explain Mr. Valentyne."

"I suppose I do, but I should probably have a lawyer."

"You will Mr. Valentyne, you will." "Alright then, what's next?"

"Can you walk?" "I think."

"Good."

"Is she ok?"

"If you mean the girl from the flower bed, then yes, she's ok."

I smile, hiding it, looking to the floor.

He un-cuffs me, first my feet and then my wrists, and he takes five very short steps backward. Another officer stands up and throws me a one-piece dark grey jumper.

"Put it on."

I smile and nod.

Whatever sedatives they have me on keep me quite content with my current situation, considering that even with Sketch dead, the company lives, and that means this is far from over. But those feelings sit behind the drugs.

After I'm dressed, they put the cuffs back on my wrists and back on my ankles. They walk me, shackles and all, down the hospital hallway and now with a count they're five cops escorting me. Into the elevator, the drugs begin to dissipate as I've lost my taste for contentment.

With everything that happened, how do I know these guys are who they appear to be?

Well, I don't.

"So how did you do it?"

One of them chirps as the others grow awkward, "Do what?"

"Fake your death? I mean you see that shit in movies, but it doesn't work in the real world."

"I didn't fake my death, someone else did." "Oh yeah, who?"

"Would you even believe me?"

They all look at each other and then the talkative one looks at me awaiting an answer.

"That's what I thought."

We reach the ground level and head out the main doors of the hospital and on to a small light grey bus, my new vehicle, to the back of it, where they lock me in the rear attached cage. Down the familiar roads of the city, I used to live in, they drive me to the station and from the bus I go, into the station, and into an interrogation room where my lawyer waits.

Hour after hour and question after question brings them nothing except my silence. The difference between this interrogation and my last one is I'm guilty and they have evidence to convict me.

This time I'm not a free man, this time they have everything they need to put me away except motive, which they don't get, because the motive lies with my excommunication from the company, and I can't explain or convince them that an insurance company is more than just an insurance company and it will do more harm than help.

Grim Associations would be a fictional element in this case, and they'll be untouched by the long arm of the law for now, and I say for now because now there is an investigation. The investigation of me, and hopefully, somehow, I'll lead them to the company but it's doubtful, because I can't claim that kind of story. They won't find any connection between Mr. Sketch, the company, and I, because there isn't one.

Police will tell you there is always a paper trail; well in this case, they're wrong because Sketch and I weren't attached by paper, we didn't have resumes or pay-cheques. We didn't have employee IDs or cubicles. We didn't have timecards or weekly shifts. We just had money deposited through different accounts and I don't even remember my account or how they contacted me. They won't find the bodies of the men I killed at the diner, maybe they'll find Charlie, or maybe Charlie and the diner have already been wiped clean, and maybe they'll stick me with that as well.

But they don't mention the diner or the pharmaceutical factory, to my surprise, because I left both places behind without thought of collecting my presence. All of the death and all of the destruction left unmentioned which could've aided in my conviction hasn't been applied and I can only guess why.

They tell me I would be charged with murder in the first degree if they could identify the body they found in my old house, and the list of charges against me continues to grow. So far, it's destruction of public property, reckless endangerment, first and second-degree arson, and finally, fraud.

My lawyer tries to persuade lesser terms, but they have a case, and I don't speak up. They propose a confession to bring leniency from the judge, but I decline because I don't believe I've done anything wrong. What is there to confess? So, I continue the silent treatment.

They prepare to transfer me to prison after deciding the trial date, and my lawyer tries to get me to speak up, but we've been here before. So, with the charges and papers they prepare to escort me from the interrogation and my lawyer, upset and rattled, tries to convince me he'll get me out of this.

But he's just as powerless as I am this time. My lawyer is escorted out and as he leaves, a different officer, not dressed in uniform but street clothes, comes in and casually sits in front me,

"I'm detective Clayton. Listen John, this silence isn't helping us and it's definitely not helping you or your case. Do you have anything to say, anything at all?"

I look at the other cops and look back at him, he turns and motions for them to leave.

"Off the record?" "Of course, John." "Call me Johnny."

"Alright, Johnny, what happened?"

"The man you're trying to identify, I know him as Benjamin Sketch. I don't know who he was before we met, and I don't really know much else about him other than that he got exactly what he deserved. Do you have my personal effects? Like my phone, or a brown envelope marked with the initials G.A?"

"We have the phone, it's damaged but it still works, but there is no envelope."

"Doesn't matter, listen, I can't prove anything to you. My innocence or guilt doesn't matter. If

you want the truth and you want answers, start with the phone. That's if it's still in your evidence room."

"I don't understand Johnny, let me help you, just help me understand."

"I can't, if you have my phone then it's a good start to your investigation."

"Johnny, I can help you, if you just start from the beginning."

"I can't."

"Give me something, Johnny." "Henry Alrick."

"Henry Alrick?"

"That's also a good place to start."

He looks at me, waiting for more, but I look away and shake my head.

"Are we done?"

"Yeah Johnny, we are."

He gets up and knocks at the door. A moment later, officers come in and help me stand.

As I walk past Detective Clayton, I smile.

Confused, he says something to one of the other cops and he escorts me elsewhere.

I don't know why I trusted detective Clayton but his willingness to understand and his sincerity convinced me. Right or wrong, I'll know soon enough.

One of the cops informs me that I get to make a phone call. I let him lead the way to the phone and I sit down knowing exactly who I'm going to call.

I dial Jess and the phone rings, rings, and rings before going to voicemail.

I sigh at the sound of her voice, after the beep, I'm silent because I've no idea what I'm supposed to say, so I stop thinking, and talk.

"I know you've waited a long time, but I need you to wait a little longer. I love you, Jess."

I hang up and the patient officers bring me to the other heavily armed officers waiting to escort me.

They walk me through the station, through the holding cells and out the back door. Out into the morning glow they help me on to the little grey bus and put me back into the cage. The escort detail has less than it did when we left from the hospital. Instead of five now, it's been cut down to three. I stay silent as they get into their places, buckling in.

They tell me the drive to the prison is three hours.

They tell me if I want to get some rest I should do it now.

All I do is stare out the window. Whether I like it or not I'm yet again a prisoner, but at least I know I am this time. The bus starts and we leave the small station behind.

Chained to a cage, my legs with barely enough room to move and my hands locked to a solid steel looped chain, I slump back in my seat and stare out.

The dawn to the longest night of my life finally arrives. I look up from my cage and out the badly tinted reinforced plexiglass windows. My eyes are barely able to stay open, but they do, and what I see is something I'll always remember, and nothing, I mean nothing will make me forget. There beyond the shitty bus windows, the ruby clouds sink into the horizon; the sun tears its way up, through the white, through the grey, and pushing away the black. I watch patiently as the night retreats, and the day is born. This is how a "vacation" is supposed to start.

But this isn't a vacation, and it never was. I was here to go home but never got to stay.

The bus barrels down the endless stretch, yellow short lines seem to fade into a single long one, lost in the blackness of the asphalt below. Even with my short victory, even though I got to see her, even though I had a taste of home, freedom, and revenge.

Satisfaction is again far off, leaving me with the bitter taste of things yet to be done.

One day, if I live through this, if the company doesn't find me, if they don't bury me. Maybe I'll get to go home for good. But if they still exist, if they still function, if they still can create that vicious drug, how can I go home?

Maybe I can't, but I'm always going to try regardless of what's next.

Charlie may have been right, it won't end this way, but I haven't changed my mind.

Whatever happens I'll take them apart piece by piece and that's why I'm not trying to take them down with the help of cops. There is too much red tape in their way, and there is nothing in my way, besides my current predicament, but I promise it's not forever.

Charlie wasn't wrong but it has nothing to do with who's going to win, it's about who lives in the end. Winning doesn't fit into it, but loss does. It's always been there and always will be. It's who can afford to lose more.

By noon the sun is bright, almost blinding, but I stare out despite it. I continue to squint and something metallic reflects it luminously, like taking a mirror and reflecting it directly in your eyes.

I try to focus on the object reflecting the light but at the speed where going it's hard to make out whatever it is. The light reflects from something on a road that connects to this one.

"What the fuck is this...,

Our driver is cut off mid-sentence as something slams into the front of the bus, sending us spinning off the road, toppling end over and end. I slam between both sides of my cage like a rag doll, but my restraints keep me closer than I would like. For the guards and driver, fortune didn't turn out in their favor because they're tossed viciously against the floor, slammed into the hard plexiglass and crushed against my cage.

We turn over and over, rolling into a field before landing on the left side of the bus opposite the door. The guards and driver fall limp finally and are either unconscious or dead, but I can't tell because I'm so dizzy I fight the urge to vomit.

The metal ring that held my chains to the cage has snapped but I'm still locked in the cage as I can hear people coming. As I try to stand in my shackles, I fall violently over. Attempt after attempt ends with the same result. I'm too rattled to keep my balance.

I hear a shotgun go off and the door of the bus disappears. Even though I'm disoriented, I make out three people dressed in black, wearing full- face masks. They drop down and enter the bus making their way over and around the unconscious guards and toward my cage. One of them watches over the guards, attentively, waiting for one of them to move. While one of them stops and grabs the key ring from an officer and opens the cage. I try again to stand, but the vertigo is so bad I have to fight to stay conscious.

Two of them grab me, dragging me from my cell past the guards, up and out of the bus.

They drag me through the dirt quickly, back toward the road. I can't even defend myself; I try to fight but I'm weak because the ringing in my ears gets worse with all the movement, and as we get closer to the road, I begin to realize what's happened.

The bus had been derailed from the road by an eighteen-wheeler that must have been going a speed that made the bus feel like a bug disappearing on a windshield flying down a highway. At least, after that hit, that's how I feel.

I recognize it, this truck. I refocus, as I'm dragged toward it. They stop outside of the massive truck; the front end was damaged but still intact from the collision. The truck's front end had been primitively reinforced, and the job looks like it had been done recently, as recent as yesterday, or maybe even today. One of my captors climbs inside and starts the truck, cheering, while the other fiddles with the guard's key ring before finding the right key, and then he undoes my chains and cuffs.

Suddenly, the third jumps past as I'm free and just as I sit up, she tackles me hard to the ground, with a forceful jerk she pulls me into her chest and squeezes me. I'm about to fight back but then she whispers in my ear,

"I've waited long enough, now they'll have to wait."

Her mask comes off and she kisses me hard. Her soft satin lips sweeten mine as I let go, I'm safe, bruised, and in pain, but I'm happy. She pulls away and stares at me with those eyes, those beautiful green to blue eyes that shine with a hazel sun surrounding the black pool of her pupil and they rain. She cries and begins to kiss me again.

What I wouldn't give for more moments like these. Just like most of my moments, this one is interrupted as well,

Smiling, she pulls away, "We've got to go."

Manny and Max remove their masks, smiling brightly, proud of their plan. Manny sits up in the truck revving the engine while Jess and Max help me stand up and climb into the large truck bay. Manny puts the monster in gear and pulls away in the opposite direction I was headed. We're going home, rolling steadily down the open road, watching the yellow line again become solid as it melds with speed, watching the scenery form into itself, a solid picture forms as we gain momentum.

No idea of what's next, I smile. As I fall unconscious, locked in Jess' embrace, in the company of my friends, whether we're there yet,

I'm home.

Of the many ways I could've found freedom, this may not have been the reunion I had in mind. But I mean it could be worse; I could be dead.

THE END...for now.